"Will you stay as my mother's companion?"

Tarini stared. Was she really being asked to live in the home of the man she loved?

Then realization dawned, and she asked quietly, "Because you and Baroness Frick intend to marry?"

"No!" Hugo rapped. "Thanks to your meddling that is no longer likely." At her stricken look, he continued more gently, "I'm sorry, Tarini. You weren't to know she'd return my ring that day you arranged for me to see her."

"Oh, I'm sorry!" More than her own happiness, Tarini wanted his.

"Don't be," he snarled, pride resurging. "I've been taught a valuable lesson. Never again will I allow myself to be contaminated with the mad malaise commonly known as love. But I shall continue enjoying your fair sex—on my own terms!"

MARGARET ROME
is also the author of these
Harlequin Romances

1676—THE GIRL AT EAGLES' MOUNT
1701—BIRD OF PARADIS
1776—THE ISLAND OF PEARLS
1939—THE GIRL AT DANES' DYKE
1957—VALLEY OF PARADISE
2052—BRIDE OF ZARCO
2096—THE THISTLE AND THE ROSE
2152—LION IN VENICE
2235—SON OF ADAM
2264—ISLE OF CALYPSO
2332—CHAMPAGNE SPRING
2369—MARRIAGE BY CAPTURE
2428—THE WILD MAN
2445—MISS HIGH AND MIGHTY
2464—CASTLE IN SPAIN
2487—KING OF KIELDER

and these
Harlequin Presents

58—MAN OF FIRE
62—THE MARRIAGE OF CAROLINE LINDSAY
101—THE PALACE OF THE HAWK
118—THE BARTERED BRIDE
128—COVE OF PROMISES
158—ADAM'S RIB
438—SECOND-BEST BRIDE
532—CASTLE OF THE FOUNTAINS

Valley of Gentians

by

MARGARET ROME

Harlequin Books

TORONTO • NEW YORK • LOS ANGELES • LONDON
AMSTERDAM • PARIS • SYDNEY • HAMBURG
STOCKHOLM • ATHENS • TOKYO • MILAN

Original hardcover edition published in 1982
by Mills & Boon Limited

ISBN 0-373-02513-0

Harlequin Romance first edition November 1982

Printed in U.S.A.

CHAPTER ONE

A LOUD two-toned chime rang out above the hustle and bustle of Manchester airport, warning travellers of an imminent announcement.

'Will all passengers for Swissair flight SR843 to Zurich please assemble at Gate Twenty-four!'

In spite of the fact that for two hours she had sat waiting, filled with nervous trepidation, mentally checking and re-checking all the instructions she had been given in case she should have omitted to have carried out some vital part of the procedure—arrive at the airport at least an hour before flight time; check in luggage; hand over ticket, receive boarding pass and keep it handy next to your passport; then relax, have a coffee or stroll around the shops until your flight number is called—Tarini's heart jolted, then began racing fast, causing her palms to sweat, her stomach to churn, her knees to almost buckle beneath her when she jumped to her feet, gathered up her handbag, magazine and one small piece of hand luggage, and set off in a panic-stricken rush towards the departure lounge.

It was still early morning, yet the airport was teeming with passengers—businessmen with bulging briefcases, parents shepherding children equipped for a holiday in the sun, young men and girls looking comfortably casual in the teenage uniform of tee-shirt and slim-legged denims, middle-aged couples obviously well-travelled enough to be looking slightly bored and others more elderly looking frankly nervous, yet all blessed with a sense of purpose, not one of them, Tarini felt certain, suffering the same sense of desolation, of loneliness, of sheer blind panic that had overwhelmed her the moment she had left home en route for the airport.

'Why did I allow myself to be coerced—bullied—into taking a holiday abroad on my own?' she murmured under her breath when, reaching the entrance to the departure lounge, she found it blocked by the head of a rambling queue. 'I should have refused to listen to Carol,' she decided, turning to trail the length of the arrival hall in search of the tail-end of a queue that seemed to be receding farther into the distance with each passing second. Feeling a twinge of anxiety, she quickened her steps, sensing that something had gone slightly awry, that this queue was a deviation from normal, an unforeseen obstacle to the carefully-prepared, step-by-step itinerary that she and Carol had meticulously rehearsed.

'I say, this is a bit much!' A disgruntled traveller confirmed her suspicions. 'If this queue isn't speeded up I'll miss my flight, my plane's due to take off in twenty minutes!'

Tarini's startled eyes flew down to her wrist-watch. *Her plane was due to take off in ten!*

'I suppose the civil servants are on a go-slow again.' Someone behind her heaved a sigh of resignation. 'I can't understand why they don't just strike and be done with it.'

'This hold-up has been caused by a need for stricter security,' a cheerful voice chimed in. 'Because of a bomb scare in this airport yesterday security officers have been ordered to be extra thorough when searching hand-luggage. But no one need worry,' he assured them so confidently that everyone relaxed, 'the airport authorities are bound to have foreseen this delay and altered their flight schedules accordingly, I'm certain no one is in any danger of missing his flight.'

Because the man sounded so authoritative, so convinced that he was right, Tarini ceased to worry and resigned herself to waiting patiently, even managed to daydream, slipping into one of the brown studies that so often in the past had irritated her mother: *'For heaven's sake, Tarini, how you can stand there staring into space with that idiotic half-smile on your lips while I'm suffering intolerable pain is beyond my comprehension!'*

Her breath caught in a gasp when the echo from a past filled with sleepless nights, tiring days, and an endless string of peevish recriminations jerked her back to reality.

'Are you feeling faint, my dear?' a kindly hand clutched her elbow. 'You've gone very pale . . .?' A stout, motherly woman peered down, her expression registering concern. 'As I was saying to my husband just a few minutes ago,' she nodded towards the man standing by her side, 'such a slip of a girl has no right to be travelling alone—you look frail, as if a strong gust of wind might blow you right off the airstrip.'

'I'm fine . . . really.' Tarini blushed, feeling awkward, unable to cope with kindness and concern in spite of weeks of devoted care that she had received after the breakdown that had occurred as a direct consequence of her mother's sudden death after years of being nursed through what her doctor had always insisted were purely imaginary ailments.

'Well, you know best, dearie . . .' The woman's voice trailed uncertainly as she eyed a small peaked face looking elfin beneath a smooth cap of hair, mouse-brown, with matching silk-fringed lashes, delicately drawn brows, and a mouth timid as a cloistered child's. A face indistinguishable in a crowd, yet redeemed from total plainness by a pair of startling eyes, blue as cornflowers, widely trusting, clearly honest, devoid of the guile, mistrust, and cynicism imposed by an increasingly violent and uncaring society.

'You must be a country girl.' The woman murmured her thoughts aloud.

'However did you guess?' Tarini looked so surprised the woman was unable to suppress a smile. Before she had a chance to reply the warning chimes rang out preceding a further announcement and she hesitated in order to listen.

'Will Miss Tarini Brown, the last remaining passenger for Swissair flight SR843 to Zürich, please proceed as quickly as possible to Gate Twenty-four!'

'Oh, no . . .!' Tarini choked. 'I'll never make it, there must still be a hundred people ahead of me in the queue!'

'Are you the missing passenger?' Immediately the woman nudged her husband. 'Tom, would you take this child to the front of the queue and explain that her plane is about to leave without her? I'm certain no one will object.'

No one did. In fact, once the situation had been outlined the crowd parted to make way for her; an official gave only a cursory glance at her passport before waving her in the direction of security officers who rifled swiftly through her shoulder bag and hand-luggage before speeding her on to a moving platform.

The long, empty passageway leading towards the departure gate seemed interminable. The platform seemed to be advancing little faster than a crawl, so desperately, once her knees and her breathing had steadied, she let go of the handrail and began to run. As soon as she came within sight of two grim-looking men in uniform standing with their backs to closed doors she realised that she was too late, that in spite of a much-too-early arrival at the airport; in spite of careful planning and meticulous attention to detail, she had committed the unpardonable error of missing her plane!

'Miss Tarini Brown . . .?' the elder of the two airline officials questioned coldly.

'Yes . . .' she gulped, feeling cowed as a prisoner awaiting sentence.

'Do you realise, I wonder, the expense incurred by an airline company when a flight is delayed? Have you any notion of the technicalities involved, the rules that must be strictly adhered to in order to move a plane safely out of a busy airport? The captain of your plane delayed take-off until the last possible moment, but when he was warned by

Flight Control that unless he left immediately his plane would be grounded for at least another four hours he had no choice but to give first consideration to the rest of his passengers. If you had arrived,' he flicked back his cuff to study his watch, 'just five minutes earlier you'd have made it. As it is,' he shrugged, 'you have no one but yourself to blame.'

'But I did arrive early,' she protested, 'I've been waiting in the airport lounge for hours! As soon as I heard my flight number called I made my way to the departure lounge, only to find a queue of people waiting to pass through the security check points, moving so slowly that there was no way I could get through in time.' Her troubled eyes scoured the men's faces, seeking a hint of sympathy, a glimmer of understanding.

The younger man shuffled his feet, looking uncomfortable. 'I should raise that point with the airport authorities, if I were you, Miss Brown. Unfortunately, individual airlines have no jurisdiction over delays caused by airport employees.'

'Nor will Swissair accept any responsibility for flights missed because of a change of airport policy,' the elder man interposed swiftly. 'You must appreciate, Miss Brown, that such checks are imperative for the safety of passengers and that whenever the circumstances warrant it the already stringent rules have to be further tightened. It's up to the individual passenger to ensure that he or she can accomplish all the formalities with plenty of time to spare.'

'I understand.' Tarini blinked, close to tears,

wondering why she should be feeling so dejected when only half an hour previously she had been wishing that she didn't have to go.

'Is this your first flight, Miss Brown?' The younger man enquired gently.

'It was to have been,' she corrected with unintentional irony. She squared her slim shoulders, making a brave effort to appear composed. 'But it doesn't matter, I think I'd much prefer to return home.'

Suddenly the elder man cleared his throat and surprised her by offering gruffly, 'No need to make hasty decisions, young lady.' He stooped to take charge of the bag she had placed at her feet. 'Let's go to my office and see what we can sort out.'

A badge pinned to his lapel identified him as John Smith, a very ordinary name for a man who, once the argument had settled, the recriminations were over, proved to be possessed of extraordinary qualities of efficiency, expertise, and a determination to transport one small piece of mislaid human baggage to Zürich at all cost.

It could be, Tarini mused, that he regarded any misplaced passenger on his airline as a personal affront. Yet when he ushered her into his office, saw her settled in a comfortable chair, then personally busied himself filling up a kettle to make her a cup of tea, she felt inclined to suspect that behind his crusty exterior lurked a compassionate heart. As she sat quietly in a corner, gratefully sipping tea, he and his companion began rustling through papers strewn over a large desk.

'Our only other flight to Zürich today is fully

booked,' she heard him mutter.

'What about the shuttle service?' the younger man suggested. 'There's a plane due to leave in five minutes that will get her to London in time to catch a connection to Zürich with less than two hours' delay.'

Hopefully, two heads lifted, two pairs of eyes swung in her direction. 'Could you manage an extra seventy-five pounds air fare, Miss Brown?'

Her blush of embarrassment appeared answer enough.

'On second thoughts,' swiftly Mr Smith turned back to his paper, 'there's a chance, a very *slim* chance,' he emphasised, 'that there might be one seat vacant on our next flight. Two seats have been booked in the name of Count Hugo von Triesen, but I know that he habitually makes provision for business associates who are sometimes required to make a spur-of-the-moment decision to finalise their business in Zürich. I saw him earlier in the restaurant eating alone—it's just possible,' he turned to study Tarini thoughtfully, 'that this could be one of the occasions when the spare seat he's reserved won't be required.'

The aristocratic ring of the name he had mentioned rendered Tarini petrified.

'Please don't bother,' she blurted, 'I don't want to be a nuisance to anyone!' Cup, spoon and saucer rattled between her shaking fingers as she deposited them carefully upon an adjacent table before rising to her feet with an endearing show of dignity. 'I really would much prefer to return home.'

'What about your luggage?' The younger man

cocked an enquiring eyebrow. 'It's already on its way to Zürich.'

'Oh . . .!' Tarini's mouth formed a quivering circle of dismay. 'I'd forgotten about that.'

John Smith straightened purposefully. 'I'd better telex Zürich airport and instruct the lost luggage office to take charge of Miss Brown's cases until she arrives—let's hope, on the next flight.'

She slumped back into her chair. Practically everything of value she possessed were contained within her two suitcases, new outfits rashly purchased at Carol's insistence with the small amount of money left over once her mother's affairs had been settled. She had doubted the wisdom of frittering her tiny nest-egg, but Carol had been so persuasive. 'Listen to me, Tarini,' her candid friend had urged, 'every item of clothing you have is shabby and out of date. When you return from holiday, blooming with health, I hope, your first priority will be to look for a job, which means that you'll need to look presentable. Far from being extravagant, a new wardrobe is a necessary investment that will help you gain the confidence needed to impress any prospective employer.'

She had not realised how visibly her thoughts had been betrayed upon her expressive face until John Smith prompted gently:

'Well, Miss Brown, have you reached a decision?'

'I seem to have been left with very little choice,' she swallowed hard. 'If you can get me a seat on the next plane to Zürich I shall be very grateful.'

For the following half hour she was left abandoned and ignored, a self-effacing shadow shrinking farther into her corner, wishing she could simply disappear from sight, while John Smith and his associate resumed their busy routine, not forgetting, at fifteen-minute intervals, to broadcast a polite request over the airport loudspeaker system.

'Would Count Hugo von Triesen kindly contact the Swissair desk before boarding his plane for Zürich?'

'Won't the old gentleman mind?' Tarini whispered timidly when the younger official approached within earshot.

'Old gentleman . . .?' He looked puzzled. Then when understanding dawned his mouth split into a wide grin. 'Count Hugo, do you mean? I'm certain he won't. In direct contrast to the elderly gentleman you've envisaged, the Count has earned himself a slightly rakish reputation. An astute businessman, he nevertheless ensures that a fair amount of his time is spent circulating the playgrounds of Europe. You've no need to worry, Miss Brown, I'm certain you'll find Count Hugo well ingrained with the aristocratic traditions of his race—that he's a gallant, ever ready to come to the rescue of a maiden in distress.'

Instead of feeling reassured she shrank even farther into her shell, fretting over the alarming new picture the young official had just painted. She had impulsively assumed that the Count would be elderly. Her knowledge of European nobility was limited to the casual perusal of small paragraphs tucked away in the corners of newspapers and magazines, and in spite of being a devoted subject of the British monarchy she had formed an impression that throughout the rest of Europe aristocrats were almost extinct, a dying breed of elderly nobles determined to hang on to worthless titles until their last expiring breath.

When the office door was flung open every head swivelled towards the tall figure that stalked across the threshold and breezed into the centre of the room.

'Well, my friends, what is it you require of me?' Tarini's fascinated eyes caught a glimpse of black hair, bronzed features and a flashing, white-toothed grin. 'I warn you that your reason had better be important enough for me to forgive you for having been forced to cut short a delightful encounter with the lovely young American actress to whom I've just been introduced!'

Shock waves ran from the tips of Tarini's toes to the crown of her head. Cowed by the impact of his vibrant personality, she crouched unnoticed in her seat, staring at the being from another world, a world that bred self-assurance to a degree she would not have dared to emulate, a world of mountains with ski-slopes that had rendered his lean limbs tough as whipcord, movements balanced and perfectly relaxed; whose sun had tanned his skin to match the bark of trees that towered, tier upon tier, towards snow-capped peaks; whose lakes had reflected into eyes narrowed with laughter a clear green sparkle holding just a hint of the chill of melted snow; whose clefts, faces and brows of rugged rock had set the pattern for a profile refined only by pride of birth.

'We have here a lady in dire need of help, Count

Hugo,' John Smith explained with the ease of a man confident of a sympathetic hearing. 'Miss Brown's plane has left without her, and as the next flight to Zürich is fully booked we're all hoping that—as has happened occasionally in the past—one of the two seats reserved in your name might not be required.'

'You are in luck!' Following the direction of John Smith's nod, the Count spun round in search of Tarini. Slowly, his amused smile faded as he raked her limp figure curled, timid as a mouse in the presence of a sleek, green-eyed tomcat. For a split second, although his expression did not change, Tarini detected a look which no young American actress would have recognised, but which was all too humiliatingly familiar to one of the wallflowers of the world—one of those girls who are always last to find a dancing partner, whose well-meaning friends insist upon manoeuvring eligible bachelors into situations in which they are forced to pretend interest in a female discarded by others as boring and unattractive.

He bowed. 'You are welcome to make use of the spare seat, Miss Brown. The friend who was to have accompanied me has cried off at the last minute,' he told her kindly. Then with slight but obvious haste he took his leave. 'If you would please excuse me, I must return to the restaurant where my friends are waiting.'

'Thank heaven for that!' John Smith's sigh of relief when the Count had retreated from his office made her feel more than ever like an unwanted piece of baggage. 'You're a very fortunate girl, Miss

Brown, your luck's turned up buttered!'

Tarini bit her lip, forcing back the ungrateful admission that given a choice she would have preferred to walk barefoot to Zürich rather than share close proximity with Count Hugo von Triesen!

CHAPTER TWO

COUNT HUGO was the last passenger to step aboard the plane. Tarini, her boarding pass clutched in an anxious fist, had been one of the first, and once she had settled into her seat she had sat nervously gnawing her bottom lip, watching the rest of the passengers filing along the aisle until every seat was occupied—except for the one on her immediate right.

Wondering which of the forthcoming experiences she would find most distasteful—the trauma of her first take-off or the ordeal of having Count Hugo von Triesen as a travelling companion—she tried to relax, forcing clenched fists to unwind until slim, pale hands appeared to be resting placidly in her lap; forcing back a tide of panic, attempting to blot from her mind the stories she had heard of horrific plane crashes that invariably seemed to occur at the most danger-prone times of landing or taking off.

A tall figure appeared in the aisle, blocking her view of the rest of the passengers while, with unhurried ease, he slid a sheaf of papers from a leather briefcase, then snapped shut the lock before stowing it on an overhead rack. She dared to meet his eyes when he slid into the adjacent seat and was not surprised to find his glance cool, his nod of acknowledgement briefly disinterested.

Then a powerful, throbbing hum began reverberating through the aircraft, a hum that developed into a whine as the plane began moving forward. As its wheels began moving faster and faster along the airstrip the whine gave way to a demoniacal shriek that sounded to Tarini like the screams of a thousand demented devils gleefully anticipating her destruction. Pressure like the force of a huge invisible hand pinned her back against her seat, then as the aircraft lifted from the ground her stomach rose with it, her body felt weightless, her brain numbed by a steady, insistent drumming in her ears.

She must have gasped aloud, or perhaps her stony immobility communicated her fear to Count Hugo, for his eyes swivelled in her direction.

'Holy Saints,' he muttered, 'you look terrified out of your wits! Is this your first flight, Miss Brown?'

The irritable snap of words attacked her pride, making it surface until it swamped every other emotion. 'Yes,' she admitted, white to the lips, 'but I'm all right now.'

She glimpsed a glint of gold, the stark contrast of a spotless cuff against a tanned, sinewed wrist when his hand lifted to summon a stewardess. She felt almost sorry for the girl at the receiving end of a smile that could have charmed a cooing dove away from its mate.

'Would you fetch a cognac, please? My . . . er . . . friend is not feeling too well. Make it two,' he amended, flashing the bemused girl a charming grin, 'I think any drink tastes better when taken in company, don't you agree?'

'Not for me, thank you,' Tarini protested weakly. 'I don't drink, even shandy goes straight to my head.'

'Please allow me to know what is best for you.' He squashed her protest with an arrogance she found infuriating. 'I can't remember how I felt on my first flight, it is so long ago, but I can imagine that one's first introduction to screaming jet engines could be quite alarming. Here, take this, and sip it slowly.' He smiled his thanks to the pretty young stewardess who had returned like a homing pigeon to his side, carrying two glasses of cognac on a tray. 'It will do you no harm, and even if it should make you feel a little tipsy,' he concluded dryly, 'the company of a person drunk on wine is preferable to one who is drunk on virtue.'

If the remark had been made purposefully snide, cleverly calculated to fire her ashen cheeks with anger, to light a spark of resentment in wide frightened eyes, the ploy succeeded. Cupping the bowl of the glass in hands shaking with indignation, Tarini tossed back her head and gulped every drop down before handing him the empty glass with the prim observation.

'Thank you, you've been very kind. Please carry on with your work,' she glanced pointedly at the sheaf of papers he had abandoned, 'I'm feeling fine now.'

She told herself that his impatient attitude justified the lie. Nothing would have induced her to admit that the horrible-tasting cognac was blazing a fiery trail from the tip of her tongue, past a pulsating throat, along every vein and nerve, threatening an explosion somewhere deep inside of her—a soundless explosion that occurred without her knowledge some minutes later, leaving behind the devastating after-affects of a head that seemed to have begun floating inches higher than her body and a tongue that began babbling an endless stream of confidences into the ear of a resigned-looking, slightly amused Count.

'I didn't want to come on holiday alone, but my friend Carol insisted. You see, my mother died recently,' to her surprise she discovered that for the very first time since her death she could think of her mother without feeling the slightest twinge of guilt, 'she'd been ill for years—not seriously ill, her doctor always insisted—just plagued every day with a different niggling complaint. The shock of her sudden death made me ill and this holiday, Carol assures me, will put me back on my feet, help me to become fit enough to find a job.'

'You have my sympathy, Miss Brown.' The Count's voice, though strangely distant, sounded gravely gentle. 'I, too, know how it feels to possess—or rather to be possessed—by an ailing, lovable, yet often infuriating mother who I suspect is not above manipulating her frailty in the pursuit of her own ends. No one knows better than she how effectively a threatened heart attack can bring a wayward son to heel.'

'Or how to wring one's conscience with the pathetic cry that the old are unwanted!' Tarini capped triumphantly.

'Or to make one feel secretive unless one takes the trouble to explain in detail about every chance encounter, every trivial happening experienced outside of the home,' he agreed with a conspiratorial grin.

Suddenly they were smiling at each other like friends revelling in the relief of shared confidences.

As they ate what Tarini considered to be a delicious meal of fruit juice, followed by roast pork and a selection of vegetables served piping hot in deep foil dishes, the effect of the cognac began wearing off so that she no longer felt lightheaded or giddy but simply cocooned within a warm golden glow that gave her the confidence to believe that the Count was not merely pretending an interest in her well-being when he probed.

'What sort of work will you choose to do once you have completely recovered from your illness, Miss Brown?'

She deliberated, scooping tiny helpings of trifle on to her spoon in the manner of a child seeking to make a treat last as long as possible.

'I shan't be in a position to choose, Count; I'm completely untrained—except perhaps as a sort of nurse-companion to the elderly—so I shall be grateful for any job with a salary sufficient to cover the expense of sharing a flat with my friend.'

'You have had to sell your home?' He looked shocked, as if such poverty was completely beyond his comprehension.

'Our house was rented,' she sighed, 'and the right of tenancy died with my mother. We ought to have been able to purchase our own home,' she frowned, 'but my late father who was a professor of Roman History and quite a brilliant scholar had no head for finance, I'm afraid. It was he who christened me Tarini . . .' The Count paused halfway in the act of raising a coffee cup to his lips, his eyes fixed upon the dreamy smile that had transformed her elfin features into a cameo of gentle serenity.

'. . . I think,' she continued musing as if to herself, 'that he must have taken one look at his unprepossessing offspring and decided to make up for what was lacking by bestowing a name of unique interest. Tarini,' she told him without the slightest trace of self-pity, 'was purported to be a Roman goddess of unusual beauty.'

'I think you do your father an injustice, Miss Brown.' Suddenly the Count sounded sorely tried. 'Why can't women learn to take compliments at face value instead of trying to read into them far more than was originally intended? Your sex is never satisfied, always you want more, more, more! *Do ut des*,' he quoted cynically. 'The code by which most women live—I give to thee so that thou givest to me!'

The flight lasted for less than two hours, yet by the time the captain's voice broadcast a warning that the plane was about to land Tarini felt she had endured a short lifetime in the Count's morose company. Obviously, she thought, the man was nursing a grievance against everyone of her sex—

not because of his mother, she felt certain, because in spite of his condemnatory remarks she had recognised a thread of deep affection running through his words, an attitude of resigned acceptance of the whims and idiosyncrasies of a beloved parent. Yet it hardly seemed possible that such an exceptionally good-looking and eligible man could have been crossed in love. In her role as an onlooker she had discovered that most girls fell like ninepins beneath the spell of an attractive rogue, that they considered character and warmth of personality to be of secondary importance to that vital component: sex appeal.

'Can you manage to fasten your seatbelt?' The Count's humour appeared almost restored to normal when warning lights flashed, prior to landing.

'I haven't *unfastened* it,' she confessed simply.

'Such an attitude is typical of your race, Miss Brown.' The set of his lips was derisory. 'Only one of the unpredictable English would scramble aboard an unfamiliar jet plane and then sit hugging an imaginary parachute!'

Yet in spite of the fact that he seemed to find her a nuisance, he was kind enough, once the wheels of the screeching jet had taxied to a standstill, to escort her into the arrival hall and shepherd her through the airport formalities. As his only piece of luggage was the briefcase he had carried aboard the plane, they were spared the chore of joining the rest of their fellow passengers clustered around a carousel that was disgorging baggage from the hold of the aircraft, so with his hand cupping her elbow he guided her in the direction of the lost property office, where John Smith had assured her she would find her two precious suitcases.

'You'll need the ticket for the flight you missed to provide means of identification,' he reminded her as they stepped up to a counter where an attendant was waiting.

Conscious of the Count's darkening frown and the attendant's growing impatience, Tarini fumbled in her handbag, then pounced with relief upon the elusive ticket, waving it like a banner beneath their distant noses.

'It's here!' she gulped. 'For one awful moment I thought I'd lost it.'

With the look of a man anxious to be relieved of his last debt to society, the Count lifted each of the retrieved cases as if it were featherlight and began striding towards a taxi rank.

'At which hotel in Zürich are you staying, Miss Brown?' While he was speaking he glanced idly at one of the labels attached to the handle of each suitcase then halted so suddenly she cannoned straight into him. She sensed that the impact of their collision was not entirely responsible for the look of shock she saw stamped upon his face when he lifted his eyes from the luggage label.

'Malbun . . .' he spelled out harshly. 'Your destination is Malbun, in *Liechtenstein*?'

When she responded with a fearful nod he breathed in deeply. 'Then how, might I ask, do you intend getting there? Taking into account the number of trains and buses that will be needed to transport you to the Swiss border and then finally to a village situated five thousand feet high in the mountains, I estimate that the journey could take at least twenty-four hours—provided, that is,' he stressed harshly, 'you miss none of your connections.'

He forbore to press the point that she had already managed to miss her plane, but her insight into his thoughts sent two hectic patches of colour flying high in her cheeks. Feeling enormous satisfaction, she hastened to put the arrogant Count firmly in his place.

'You've been very kind, Count von Triesen, and I'm extremely grateful to you for helping me over a difficult period, but as from this moment you need feel no further responsibility on my behalf. Mr Smith telephoned personally to the office of the tour operators with whom I booked my holiday and in turn they passed on to him the telephone number of a courier in Zürich who has been instructed to deal with all further travelling arrangements. So you see, you may leave me now without suffering the least twinge of conscience.' Deliberately she stuck out her hand. 'Goodbye—or rather,' she blushed slightly, 'now that we're in your country it seems more appropriate to say: *auf Wiedersehen*!'

'You have the telephone number written down? Give it to me. . . .' To her consternation he ignored her outstretched hand completely.

'Really, there's no need. . . .'

'You are *au fait* with the intricacies of foreign telephone exchanges?' he questioned sharply.

'Well . . . no, but I'm certain I'll be able to manage.'

'As well as you've managed up until now, I've no doubt.' The dry observation left her seething. 'Come,' once again he grabbed her by the elbow and began propelling her in the direction of a nearby telephone kiosk, 'a few more minutes of precious time will be well spent ensuring that you are to be deposited in capable hands.'

For the first time in her uneventful life Tarini felt an urge to rant and rave. But knowing that such a reaction would be futile, that the dictatorial Count had no intention of being shaken off, she submitted to being led into a telephone kiosk and stood quietly simmering while he dialled the required number.

'You're through . . .' When a voice responded to his enquiry he handed her the receiver, but instead of stepping out of earshot he remained grimly listening.

'H . . . hello,' she gasped, 'this is Tarini Brown speaking. I was instructed by the tour operators to contact you immediately I arrived in Zürich.'

'Oh, yes, Miss Brown.' The girl's reply was so politely offhand Tarini's nerves tightened.

'I believe you may be able to help me,' she almost pleaded, 'I need transport to my hotel in Malbun.'

'Certainly I can help you.' To her relief the courier responded with alacrity. 'But I'm afraid it's out of the question for me to accompany you because in an hour's time I'm due to pick up a plane load of tourists who are en route for Lake Lucerne. This duty must have been overlooked by my head office when they promised you an escort and wired instructions to me to meet your plane. However, I have enquired on your behalf about which train to catch, and also the times of a series of connecting buses that will get you to Triesenberg, which is as far as local buses run. Once you get there, it should not be difficult to contact the village taxi driver who will take you on the last stage of your journey up the mountain to the ski resort of Malbun. Have you a pencil and paper handy?'

Numb with shock, Tarini fumbled in her handbag for a notebook and pencil. 'Yes,' she croaked, 'I have now.'

'Right!' Sounding relieved to have been spared a spirited argument, the courier began rattling off a list of train and bus schedules. 'Remember, T-R-I-E-S-E-N-B-E-R-G, she spelled out plainly, 'marks the last stage of your journey,' she stressed before she finally concluded, 'Have a pleasant journey, I'm certain you'll cope beautifully.'

When the line went dead Tarini slowly replaced the receiver and remained staring fixedly at the name of a village that seemed vaguely familiar.

'Triesenberg? Of course!' her eyes flew upwards to her companion's face. 'Count von Triesen—Triesenberg. What a coincidence!'

'Hardly that, Miss Brown.' The Count sounded savagely resigned. 'As it did not seem important at the time, I did not bother to correct your assumption that I am Swiss. I am, in fact, a subject of the Principality of Liechtenstein, and the village of Triesenberg is just a few kilometres from the Schloss Wolke, which has been the home of my family for centuries.'

Suddenly, fatigue descended like a cloud upon a frail body that only weeks ago had fought a brave battle to survive an illness caused by exhaustion, by years of selfless dedication to the impossible task of ministering to an invalid whose demands had grown heavier and more fractious with each passing day. An hysterical desire to laugh rose within her as she recalled her doctor's parting advice.

'What you need now, Tarini, is a holiday, a restful interlude in some place that can provide fresh, clean air and gentle exercise, plenty of good wholesome food to put flesh on your bones and above all, a peaceful environment, for you must avoid at all cost any situation that might cause you stress!'

What would he think of the situation she was in now? she wondered, subconsciously tightening her grip until her knuckles whitened around the flimsy slip of paper that was to be her only guide across a width of unknown territory whose inhabitants spoke a language foreign to her ears. Would the dear old physician who had done his best to ease the burden that had been forced upon her the day she had left school and had not been shed until two days after her twentieth birthday advise her to return home immediately? Or would he censure her, as he had done previously, for her timidity, for reacting to adverse circumstances with the resignation of a child who, having been told continually that she is unloved and unlovable, begins accepting tribulation as a penance?

'Don't fret, Miss Brown, I'm certain it can be doing you no good.' The Count sounded calm, his eyes surprisingly kind as they rested upon white teeth gnawing a tortured bottom lip. Reaching for the crumpled piece of paper she was grasping like a lifeline, he plucked it from her grasp and with a gesture of distaste threw it in a handy waste receptacle. 'I shall be travelling to Liechtenstein first thing in the morning,' he forestalled her outraged gasp, 'it would be criminally selfish of me, don't you think, if I were to allow a visitor to my country to endure unfamiliar trains and buses while keeping a speedy, comfortable car all to myself?'

CHAPTER THREE

CAREFULLY, Tarini laid her modest nightdress across smooth, flower-sprigged bed sheets, then stepped back frowning, disturbed by the incongruity of limp white poplin spread against a luxurious pillow and a plump, featherlight, matching duvet. Of course it was out of place—but then so was she! She had been given no chance to argue, no chance even to catch her breath before being whisked into a taxi and sped through the streets of Zürich towards an hotel whose magnificence, when she had been ushered into the foyer, had reduced her to a shrinking, tongue-tied shadow who had yearned to be allowed to sink through the cream marble floor sparkling mirror-bright beneath the soles of her dusty shoes; to melt into walls lined with black plate glass reflecting elegant potted palms, banked flower arrangements, huge crystal chandeliers, and an imposing reception desk presided over by a concierge whose imperturbable expression had not altered one iota when the Count had requested that a room should be found on the same floor as his own for the waif trailing nervously in his wake.

He had not been unkind enough to use those specific words, of course, but the pageboy's sympathetic grin when he had shown her inside a lift that had swooshed her silently up to the highest, most prestigious floor of the hotel had contained a message of recognition from a kindred spirit, one who knew how it hurt to feel inferior, one who had no difficulty interpreting awe, humility, and downright panic in her dilated stare.

Tarini's heart lurched with fright when a telephone shrilled its summons through the silent room. Nervously, she started towards it, then hesitated, her hand hovering over a handset of pale green onyx banded with gilt. But when the insistent trill became more than her nerves could stand she plucked it from its rest and quavered into the mouthpiece.

'H . . . hello. . . .?'

'Miss Brown, you sound distressed, is anything wrong?' the Count questioned sharply.

'N . . . no, everything's fine,' she gulped, then in case he should think her ungrateful, hurriedly qualified: 'My room is comfortable, and so luxuriously furnished it's quite taken my breath away.'

'Good.' She could tell by his tone that he was smiling. 'Instinct tells me that for too long you have wallowed in the luxury of martyrdom, therefore it is time you were forced to endure the misery of a little spoiling. If you are not feeling too tired, would you care to join me for dinner this evening?'

'Oh, but . . .' She began scrabbling in her mind for words of refusal.

'Don't bother to change,' he continued briskly, ignoring her obvious confusion, 'have a quick wash and brush up and I'll meet you downstairs in fifteen minutes.'

When the line clicked and then went dead she stood staring stupidly, frozen with dismay at the prospect of having to venture down an imposing staircase and to pretend to be relaxed enough to force morsels of food past a throat so tight she could barely manage to swallow. Then his imperious command impinged upon her conscience. *'I'll see you downstairs in fifteen minutes.'*

How on earth did he expect her to eliminate the grime and creases of a journey that had commenced during the early hours of this morning, within the short space of fifteen minutes!

The threat of attracting his displeasure sent her scurrying towards suitcases lined up against a wall in readiness for their early-morning departure. Luckily, her hand-luggage, a small vanity case accommodating make-up and toiletries, also contained a spare pair of tights, a change of underwear, and a blouse bought as an afterthought, which she had tucked inside the pocket lining of her case at the very last minute.

Relieved by the knowledge that her leaf-green woollen suit had stood up to the journey well, she sped into the bathroom for a rapid shower and emerged ten minutes later from a cloud of steam looking pink-cheeked and breathless but feeling vastly refreshed.

The blouse, when it settled across her shoulders with a soft, silken sigh, amply condoned her last guilty extravagance by enclosing tilted breasts and a tender stem of neck within pink rose-petal folds, its billowing sleeves lending an illusion of roundness to too-slender arms; ruffled cuffs disguising the fragile, sparrow-boned thinness of her wrists. Just a light application of make-up, a touch of colour on lips that had to be forcibly held still, a few strokes of a comb through her hair, and she was physically ready—but still mentally unprepared. Her wristwatch told her that she was five minutes late when she hurried into a lift that sped her swiftly down to the foyer to face yet another intimidating hurdle—a downward sweep of staircase giving access to two rooms, a dining-room to the left where silver cutlery glistened against a pristine background of white damask tableclothes thrown over innumerable small tables being attended by an army of soft-footed waiters, and to the right, a lounge bar bathed in subdued lighting, with opulent chairs and couches grouped in its centre and ranged around its walls, and low tables some supporting silver buckets holding dark green bottles plunged into cracked ice, with a folded napkin swathed around each frosted neck.

Count Hugo had drawn her a quick verbal sketch

of the layout of the hotel, but his words had barely registered. Certainly, nothing he had said had prepared her for a magnificence she found terrifying. Willing her footsteps not to falter, she negotiated the last few steps, then stood rooted before closed glass doors, knowing that nothing on earth could induce her to enter the vast dining-room alone.

Giving in to cowardice, she spun on her heel to make a quick retreat, but even as her foot descended upon the first marble stair a mocking remark speared from somewhere behind her.

'You bore a large misfortune with great courage, Miss Brown, why weaken now in the face of what is by comparison a very minor venture?'

Reluctantly she turned to face the Count. 'Sometimes it takes courage to admit to cowardice, Count Hugo,' she husked. 'Will you take pity on my timidity and excuse me from joining you for dinner—I'd much prefer to have something light served in my room?'

'No, I will not excuse you, nor will I take pity upon one lacking in self-esteem,' he refused tersely. 'If you persist in undervaluing yourself, you cannot justly complain if you are undervalued by others. Now is as good a time as any to begin learning to mix with confidence, to discover that no one can make you feel inferior without your co-operation and consent!'

For a second she looked stricken, then pride squared her slim shoulders, tilted her head to betray in the depths of flower-blue eyes a glint of long-lost spirit.

'Very well, Count Hugo,' she bowed to the inevitable, 'if you insist.'

A smile of satisfaction quirked his lips as he reached for her hand and tucked it within the crook of his elbow.

'You're looking quite pretty this evening,' he encouraged, dallying on the threshold of the dining-room to enjoy the wild blush of colour rioting in her cheeks. 'What is it about the delicate English rose, I wonder,' he sounded genuinely puzzled, 'that makes every other flower appear vulgar, and too colourfully flamboyant by comparison?'

Although the compliment was an obvious ploy to boost her confidence, it nevertheless prompted a glow that lasted right throughout dinner, a light meal of clear soup, lake trout and salad, followed by a helping of chestnut mousse which, though it looked and tasted delicious, she accepted only because the Count was so persuasive.

'You really must eat more,' he remarked, studying delicate features that seemed to be altering every few seconds according to the whim of a low candle flickering inside a circle of flowers set on the table between them; one moment steady, casting a veil of calm serenity, and the next animated by a slight movement of air, throwing shadows under high cheekbones, tremors over a young, vulnerable mouth, drawing a screen of secrecy over dark blue eyes whose candid look he had begun to recognise as her trademark.

'I've never been blessed with a large appetite,' she confessed, resisting an impulse to fidget when his stare became intent, 'but I must be improving, for the meal I've just enjoyed is the largest I've eaten since my illness.'

'You must try to do better than that, or else risk offending the proprietress of your hotel in Malbun.'

'I'm looking forward to living on top of a mountain,' she responded eagerly, 'I can hardly wait to get there.'

'You appear to be imagining your hotel perched high on a mountain peak.'

'Isn't it?'

He laughed aloud at her look of disappointment. 'Not quite. The Hotel Rothus, where you will be staying, is situated five thousand feet high, but in a sheltered valley with snow-capped peaks towering all around it. It is used mainly as a ski lodge and is packed with winter sports enthusiasts right throughout the winter season. But gradually, over the years, the holiday season has been extended to include the summer months also. This month, May, must be the quietest of all, yet many would argue that springtime in the Alps is the most beautiful of all the seasons. In spite of the fact that your hotel will not have its full complement of guests, that there will be no hordes of ravenous skiers descending upon her dining-room, the proprietress, whom I know well, is certain to be upset if any of her guests does not do justice to the hearty soups floating with dumplings, the pancakes, the boiled beef and saddles of venison and chamois, the strudel, soufflés and gâteaux for which she is justly famous.'

'You make my holiday sound as if it might turn out to be a feat of gastronomic endurance,' she protested faintly. 'I couldn't sample half the things you've mentioned—one suet dumpling would satisfy my appetite for the better part of a week!'

'Ah, but wait until you have spent a full day in invigorating Alpine air,' he nodded wisely. 'After a few hours spent walking the peaks I'm willing to bet that you will quickly change your tune. Did your doctor advise you to visit the Alps in order to reap the benefits of clear mountain air and good wholesome food?'

Forgetting to be shy, Tarini leant forward to confide, 'The choice of location was entirely mine. For years I've promised myself that if ever I were to be lucky enough to take a holiday abroad my destination would be Liechtenstein. Snatches I've read about the tiny principality overshadowed by its larger neighbours, Germany, Switzerland, and Austria yet somehow managing to retain its independence and culture, caught my imagination, made me yearn to see for myself the castle of the reigning prince, the lonely, untouched world of the Alps, the flower-filled meadows, the cows with tinkling bells hung round their necks, and to soak up the atmosphere—for almost every paragraph I've read about your country has referred to it as: the valley of peace.'

She seemed so steeped in romantic wonderment he hesitated, as if loath to damage the dream she nurtured.

'Twenty years ago my country could possibly have been used as a background for an operetta,' he told her cautiously, 'for then it really was a valley of peace with cows wandering along the streets of a capital that is now packed with buses and cars. Modern houses cover slopes that once were spread only with flowers. Factory buildings are scattered throughout the valleys, and high up in what you referred to as the lonely and untouched world of the Alps, ski lifts, chalets and hotels abound. Liechtenstein has awoken from its long sleep, Miss Brown, the fairy tale atmosphere that was prevalent in the old days is now as illusory as your highly romantic image.'

He winced from a look reminiscent of a child who has just been told that there is no Father Christmas.

'So you no longer have a reigning prince living in an historical castle?'

'Oh, yes, we have a Prince,' he seemed relieved to be able to reassure her on one point at least. But impelled by a duty to be honest, he qualified: 'However, his castle has now been transformed into a modern home where the Prince and Princess live in a happy atmosphere of simplicity with their five children. Our monarch has often made plain his dislike of superficial pomp and ceremony, which is why there is no court etiquette and why he is rarely in uniform. He insists upon his family mixing with his subjects on very democratic and friendly terms—even to the point of sending his children to the local school in the capital, Vaduz, for the first years of their education.'

'Oh, I see . . .' Though she strove to appear unconcerned her voice was bleak with disappointment.

Looking uncharacteristically sympathetic, he attempted to redress the balance. 'Perhaps it is we Liechtensteiners who have changed more than our actual surroundings. I suspect, Miss Brown, that one as convinced as you appear to be that paradise exists is sure to find it. Perhaps it could still be lurking beneath the surface, and once you move away from the towns and into the country you may still discover your own particular valley of peace waiting for you somewhere in the mountains. But meanwhile,' he reverted to briskness, 'the mountains must wait until the nightlife of Zürich has been explored!'

As their hotel was central they decided to walk rather than take a taxi, meandering slowly along streets lined with shops crammed with goods of every description, their window displays so eye-catching and original Tarini's mouth was soon in danger of setting into a permanent circle of delighted astonishment. Jewels, watches and furs; clothing for comfort and sport, for leisure and for glittering nights out on the town; antiques and objets d'art; books, exotic food and mouthwatering confectionery; embroidery, lace and hand-carved wooden animals made it almost impossible to decide upon a souvenir.

But it was when they came to the river and began strolling along a bank lined with guildhouses, curious boutiques and many enticing-looking side streets that she really began to soak up the gay, cosmopolitan atmosphere of Switzerland's largest city.

'Would you like a drink?'

She was about to refuse until Count Hugo indicated with a nod a pavement café looking on to the river, its tables topped by colourfully striped umbrellas, its chairs filled with youngsters who could have been students wearing a uniform of faded, skin-tight denims, tee-shirts stamped with slogans, and with the inevitable guitars slung across some of their shoulders.

'I'd love a Fanta,' she decided, noting a large number of the fruit juice cans strewn across the students' tables.

'Are you sure you wouldn't like an iced lollipop to go with it?' he drawled sarcastically, then relented immediately he saw her humiliated blush. 'Forgive that boorish remark,' he apologised quickly, 'of course, you may drink whatever you wish.'

As boats sailed past on a river reflecting the brilliance of strings of coloured fairy lights; as the fragrance of linden trees filled the air and somewhere behind her someone began strumming a guitar, Tarini's hurt faded, the embarrassment caused by the Count's puzzling jibe superseded by a glow that she eventually began to recognise as the elusive, long-lost stranger in her life-supreme contentment.

Count Hugo ordered a bottle of wine for himself and when it was brought to their table he tried to tempt her to taste a few sips.

'It is very light, a Clevner wine which must always be drunk chilled, made from blue Burgundy grapes grown on the shores of Lake Zürich. Try a little, it will do you no harm . . .'

'No, thank you,' she refused hastily, 'Alcohol, however much diluted, always has a curious effect upon my tongue and I've no intention of boring you with the story of my life, as I'm afraid I did during our plane journey. I'd far rather hear about your life,' she dared to display shy curiosity, 'it's such a novelty for me to be in the company of a sophisticated man of the world.'

'Is that how I appear to you?' He looked mildly amused.

'Of course,' she confirmed simply. 'You must be aware that your privileged upbringing has endowed you with an air of self-assurance rarely achieved by ordinary mortals who lack the status of a title and the rarefied background of a stately home. And as if that were not enough to excite anyone's envy,' she sighed, 'you also possess more than your fair share of physical attraction. All the good fairies must have been present at your christening, Count Hugo. Undoubtedly, you are one of Fortune's favourites—a man who has everything!'

'At the risk of sounding trite, I must remind you that appearances can often be deceptive.' She was surprised to see a scowl darkening his features and jumped nervously when, pushing his glass aside, he suddenly bit out: 'As you seem to pride yourself on an ability to judge character, Miss Onlooker-who-sees-most-of-the-game, perhaps you could come up with a theory that might explain why a man such as you have just described—one who has everything and could therefore presumably be regarded as the answer to any maiden's prayer—should have recently been jilted?'

'Jilted? *You?*' Tarini stared, round-eyed. 'The girl, whoever she is, must be out of her mind!'

His head reared, displaying a profile etched with hauteur, his glance sharpened by the suspicion that her words had held a ring of sarcasm. But one look from honest eyes, tender with compassion, seemed to dispel the unworthy thought. Wryly, with a twist to his lips that tugged her heartstrings, he complimented dryly:

'You may lack some of the more blatant attributes regarded by many as essential to the makeup of an attractive female, Miss Brown, nevertheless you certainly know how to soothe a man's savaged ego.' Abruptly, he rose to his feet and pushed back his chair. 'Let's walk!' he commanded, at the same time extending a hand, inviting her to slip cool, slim fingers in his. Smothering a gasp of surprise, she responded to his bidding, intuitively aware that Count Hugo, the man she had dubbed a self-possessed, sophisticated man of the world, felt in need of a confidante!

Sensing that he was unused to unburdening his worries on to the shoulders of others, that the impression he gave of being in complete command of his own destiny was no façade, but rather a duty ingrained during childhood into a boy destined to become a man of authority, she made no attempt to force his confidence but strolled along the river bank with her hand clasping his, communicating silent sympathy. Then as if inspired by mental telepathy, their footsteps slowed as they crossed a deserted bridge spanning a river flowing seductive as silk, sighing a song of solitude composed especially for lovers.

'If things had worked out the way I'd hoped, your accusation of my being over-privileged would have been amply justified.' Leaning his arms against the parapet, he cast a brooding glance downwards to the river. 'I could hardly believe my luck when, after months of fruitless argument, Maria finally gave in and accepted my proposal of marriage. She's the most beautiful creature on earth,' he confided to the mysterious depth of water, 'her hair looking at times like a spun gold coronet piled high upon her head, always sweet-smelling, and fresh as the buttercups she often used as a pillow whenever we walked too far and she became fatigued. Treasured moments of bliss,' he murmured, so deep in thought Tarini felt like pinching herself to ensure that she had not suddenly been rendered invisible, 'the feel of her soft, tender body melting against mine; the thrill of a tiger-cub purr reaching from the depths of a milk-white throat; lips tasting of honey; potent, whispered promises that acted like a drug upon the senses . . .'

'What went wrong . . .?' The involuntary cry was torn from Tarini's lips.

Resenting intrusion into his privacy, he swung round to direct a glittering, green-eyed stare.

'My mother decided to interfere,' he clenched. 'Simply because Maria has been married once before, because she was courageous enough to divorce a husband who had treated her abominably, my mother refused to acknowledge her as a future daughter-in-law, thereby plunging us all into a conflict Maria found so unendurable she was forced into issuing an ultimatum. *"As much as I love you, Hugo, my darling,"* ' he intoned stonily, ' *"I can fight for you no longer. The time has come when you must decide whose happiness matters most—mine, or your mother's!"* '

'Oh!' Tarini had not meant to sound condemnatory, but her exclamation rang unmistakably with the disappointment of a romantic idealist who imposes impossibly high standards of chivalry upon her heroes, whose heroines are never allowed a Past, because their purity had to be unquestionable, white as the proverbial driven snow . . .

Her telling gasp tipped flame to his sensitive fuse.

'Damn all censorious, sanctimonious women!' he exploded, grabbing her shoulders to administer a furious shake. 'How swift you are to condemn the small indiscretions of your less fortunate sisters. Can it be,' he jeered angrily, 'that you are simply jealous of others more beautiful than yourselves, that you are forever conscious of nondescript looks that deny you both the ability to tempt and the opportunity to be tempted?'

CHAPTER FOUR

As Tarini had expected, Count Hugo's car was an opulent limousine with sparkling maroon body-work, glistening chrome fittings, plump white-walled tyres, and an interior décor of a smooth, rich shade of buttercream.

Timidly, she crouched in her seat, wishing the upholstery rippling soft as chamois leather beneath her palms would open up and swallow her completely, thereby curtailing the journey which, since they had set off half an hour previously, had developed into a silent embarrassing nightmare.

Her interest perked up when they began leaving the outskirts of Zürich behind them, factory units, warehouses, garages and blocks of flats that could have been part of any major city giving way to hedgerows, farmhouses and fields full of grazing livestock. In spite of the fact that Count Hugo's deeply morose mood had shown no sign of abating, she nerved herself to intrude upon his silence in order to resolve a problem that was causing her considerable worry.

'Count Hugo . . .' she jerked.

'Miss Brown . . .' he began simultaneously.

After a second's startled silence they both broke into laughter, his a deep-throated chuckle, hers more of a giggling, nervous gulp.

'Please continue with what you were about to

say,' he urged politely when courage appeared to have failed her.

'It's just that I'd like to settle the debt I owe you,' she dived in search of her handbag, to hide her blush of confusion. 'When I asked for my bill before leaving the hotel I was told that it had already been taken care of.'

She emerged from her search just in time to see a curl of disdain lifting the corner of his mouth. 'Please try to regard it as a small gesture of atonement, Miss Brown. I am aware that money cannot buy forgiveness, and that the payment of a small bill can in no way compensate for the boorish way I behaved last night, but if I add to it my sincere apologies will that help?'

'You were upset,' she excused in a breathless rush, 'and understandably so, considering the circumstances.'

'Thank you, Miss Brown,' he accepted gravely, offering no contradiction, 'I felt certain I could rely upon your generosity.'

'H . . . have you decided what you're going to do,' she stammered out the question that had caused her many sleepless hours, 'about your mother and your fiancée, I mean?'

The silence that followed, a glimpse of knuckles whitening as he tightened his grip upon the steering wheel, seemed to indicate that he considered the question an impertinence. Then suddenly he sighed, the weary, heartfelt sigh of a man in need of a friendly shoulder to share his burden.

'I feel like a pennant tattered by variable winds, blown first one way and then the other, in danger of being torn apart by the love I feel for my fiancée and the duty I owe to my mother. At times, I've managed to convince myself that my own happiness, and Maria's, should be my prime consideration, but as you have no doubt discovered for yourself, Miss Brown, a mother can wield duty like a whip to revive flagging conscience.'

'I know exactly what you mean,' she nodded thoughtfully, 'although I'm sure my own mother would have been offended at the thought of duty being linked with personal relations. All people, however unreasonable they may sometimes appear, need to be liked; no one, and especially not a mother, wants to feel she's the object of patient resignation.'

'Are you implying that I should be feeling grateful for being used like a pawn on my mother's chessboard?' he challenged bitterly.

'I can think of many worse things than being made a pawn of love,' she reminded him wryly. 'You take your blessings too much for granted, Count Hugo, instead of complaining about two women loving you too well, you ought to remember the many, much less fortunate, who have no one to love, no one who loves them.'

'Am I right in thinking,' his imperious eyebrows lifted, 'that you are obliquely implying that I am spoiled?'

The dangerously soft challenge filled her with confusion. She felt sympathy for him in his dilemma; no one knew better than she about the torment inflicted by a demanding parent, the querulous railing against the selfishness of youth; the pitiful fear of loneliness that blinded the aged to youth's need to be free to spread its wings, yet in spite of her compassion, she could not bring herself to lie. Mourning the fact that she seemed fated always to be prodding his dragon's temper, she ventured timidly:

'Considering your background, it would be a miracle if you weren't. I think all charming, worldly-wise people are spoiled, it's part of their charisma.'

She waited tensely for a reaction that was ominously slow in coming, then started with surprise when the silence was broken by his shout of laughter.

'Your velvet tongue could blunt the edge of a dagger, Miss Brown!' His chuckle of amusement amazed her. 'I number many diplomats among my friends, but not one of them can match your ability to castigate in such a way that your victim is made to feel grateful for the experience. You are a deceiving wench,' he decided thoughtfully, 'supple as a willow branch that can be bent but never broken.'

Tarini passed the rest of the journey in a blissful daze, conscious that some miracle had changed her morose foe into a friendly companion, yet not quite certain how it had occurred. As he supplied her with a running commentary on the changing face of the countryside her relaxation became so complete she cried out with excitement when she caught her first glimpse of a mountain lake—a brilliant ice-green splash of colour immediately obscured by a belt of trees.

'Oh, how delightful . . .!' She twisted round in her seat in an attempt to see more. 'I never imagined water could look so green.'

'The best is yet to come,' he assured her with a smile. 'Once we reach the top of this rise you will enjoy your first encounter with the Rhine Valley and the wooded slopes of the surrounding *massifs*.'

'*Massifs* . . .' she repeated slowly, enjoying the taste of the foreign word upon her tongue. 'You speak English so perfectly, Count Hugo, I have difficulty remembering that you are not one of my own countrymen.'

'English is our second language.' He took his eyes away from the road just long enough to cast a smile that stopped her heartbeats, then set them racing thunderous as a cataract down a mountain gorge. 'Liechtenstein has a patois all its own, a vocabulary that has been officially recorded yet which is not widely available in the form of a dictionary, nevertheless it is so closely associated with German that even the most uneducated peasant can interpret words spoken in that language. But you will have no difficulty making yourself understood, for even in the most remote mountain villages you would be unfortunate not to come across at least one person who could understand, if not converse, in English.'

When the car breasted a rise he braked and guided it to a standstill at the side of the road. Displaying surprising insight into her feelings, he did not attempt to intrude with speech upon a moment so profoundly moving that when he helped her out of the car she stood rooted, mesmerised by a view so awe-inspiring no film or paintbrush could hope to do it justice.

Towering granite peaks still with a frosting of winter snow reared against a backcloth of summer-blue sky, completely cloud-free, the only movement caused by the wheeling of a solitary eagle lazily policing his territory in search of a marmot to provide his next meal. Lower down on wooded slopes, dark branches tipped with spring green were swaying in the breath of a light breeze, and on the floor of a patchworked valley irrigated by a river threading a silver course past neatly cultivated fields, lush pastureland, and a scattering of tiny villages Tarini saw houses resembling cuckoo clocks from which she would not have been surprised to see birds popping from under the eaves to record in chorus each passing hour.

'Well, could this be the valley of peace for which you are searching?' he prompted softly, smiling his appreciation of an expression so rapt, so chased with emotions that words were rendered superfluous.

'I never imagined . . .' she drew a hesitant breath, 'I've seen pictures, of course, and read books describing wooden houses with carved balconies and ornamental windows and door-frames, but neither prepared me for this . . . this feeling that Heidi herself might appear in the doorway of one of those houses any moment now!'

'The local peasantry has an instinctive feeling for the sort of building material most appropriate to his surrounds,' he agreed, 'and fortunately there is an abundant supply of pine, fir, and larchwood in the forests to allow them to continue exercising the wealth of experience handed down from generations of forebears. Nevertheless, in spite of the area's Alpine image, we still have some distance to travel before we reach Heidi-land.' As he urged her back to the car his grin held more than a hint of teasing. 'For one who seems to have existed upon a diet of fairytales, Miss Brown, this view can be regarded as no more than a nibble, a starter to whet your appetite for the banquet still to come.'

During the following hour she was treated to a surfeit of views that left her gasping as they left behind them lakes shimmering satin-smooth beneath warm spring sunshine, dappled by shadows cast by towering peaks; stirred by shoals of fish clearly visible through crystal clear water; pounded here and there into a cauldron of activity by cataracts tossed like silver streamers from great heights, enveloping the lake surface in a mist of scintillating spray. As the road climbed higher she was able to examine for the first time at close quarters herds of Alpine cows the colour of pale straw, with large, doleful eyes and placid faces, each with a leather neckband sporting a large, tinkling bell.

'Less than two weeks ago the road leading to your hotel was blocked with snow,' he told her, 'but any day now the cows will be herded up to higher pastures where they will remain all during the summer. In autumn, the cowherds, in whose care they are left, will bring them back down to the valley where their owners will be anxiously waiting to find out which one of them is the proud possessor of the "queen cow", the one that has earned the right to lead the herd with an upturned milking stool tied between its horns and a coloured heart festooned across its forehead, for every Liechtensteiner yearns to be able to boast that he is the owner of the best cow of the high pastures, the one named first in her herd in yield of milk, butter, and cheese. You can tell a queen cow by the size of the bell hung around her neck—the better the yield, the larger the bell.'

As the bells she could see around the necks of the grazing herd looked cumbersome, made out of some heavy dull metal and with a clapper to provide a tinkling accompaniment to their every movement, she was moved to protest.

'I think it's most unfair to reward industry with an increased burden. Surely it should be the other way around . . .?'

'Life is never fair, Miss Brown.' She could tell by his tone that he was not taking her remark seriously. 'The world is divided into talkers and doers; invariably, it is the talker who has stood in the background keeping his hands clean, who steps into the limelight whenever there are accolades to be received.'

'Yes,' she nodded thoughtfully, 'my father used to say that if ever one needed a job done in a hurry one should always go to a man who already has too much to do.'

'Your father must have been a student of philosophy,' he grinned, 'as well as being adept at matching character with an appropriately beautiful name. May I have your permission to call you Tarini?' He glanced sideways at her startled face.

'Although, once our journey is over, we are unlikely ever to meet again, I shall think of you often, Tarini Brown—the shy, timid little English girl who was such a sympathetic listener she won from me secrets I would hesitate to confide even in a close relative. But we are friends now, aren't we?' he continued to amaze her by adding. 'In fact, given the opportunity, I think we might have become very good friends indeed, don't you agree?'

Friends! Something deep inside her baulked at the insipid word, because in spite of the fact that friendship with a man like Count Hugo was more than a nobody such as herself had any right to expect; in spite of the fact that in less than an hour he would be taking his leave of her, no doubt uttering polite expressions of regret at the unlikelihood of their ever meeting again, she knew that she was more than halfway to falling in love with him.

'Well, Tarini, you haven't answered my question . . .?' He cast her an amused glance. 'Don't tell me that you are one of those misguided souls who declare that friendship between a man and a woman is impossible?'

'There are two sorts of friendship,' her brow puckered as she sought for words to express her theory. 'On the one hand there is friendship as light and inconsequential as the brush of a butterfly's wings across a windowpane, and on the other, there is friendship that must be studied deeply as a book, because all persons are puzzles, and puzzles can't be understood until one has found the key. I imagine,' she concluded gravely, 'that most friendships between a man and a woman would fit into the first category, because basically man is an idle creature who prefers to sit back and be amused by the light and undemanding, rather than be forced to delve into the pages of a book which at first sight may appear dull but whose contents he might find rewarding.'

'What a profound creature you are!' Smoothly, he changed into a lower gear to negotiate the road, ribboned with hairpin bends, that had begun circuiting a mountain. 'Were it not for the fact that I have to leave for Austria first thing in the morning and that I'm unlikely to return before your two weeks' holiday is over, I should insist upon furthering our acquaintance. But I can at least show you my home.' He drew the car to a standstill in a layby that had obviously been designed as a vantage point from which to survey the countryside from a dizzy height.

Simply by craning her neck, Tarini could see the ribbon of road descending thousands of feet down the mountainside. Then, following his directive, she lifted her eyes to an adjacent peak and saw a belt of woodland topped by the towering grey walls of a castle with four round towers, set one at each corner, their pointed, red-tiled roofs shaped like witches hats poking the skyline.

'Schloss Wolke—Cloud Castle,' he interpreted for her benefit.

She stared up at the majestic pile that looked as if it had been growing out of the rock for centuries, thinking how aptly it had been named—Cloud

Castle—a castle in the air, a visionary project, a daydream, a splendid imagining which has no real existence, like one of the fairytale castles built at a word that could be made to vanish with equal swiftness. Childishly, she blinked, then opened her eyes wide to ensure that the castle was still standing.

'It looks very grand,' she finally managed to gulp, 'so grand that it's hard to imagine anyone actually living there.'

'It can be a feat of endurance at times,' he smiled, starting up the car to resume their journey. 'One needs time to readjust to draughty corridors and smoky fireplaces after prolonged stays in luxury hotels.'

When the road suddenly dipped Tarini's heart dipped with it, sensing as they drove down into a valley dominated by a wooden three-storied building tiered with balconies running beneath mosaic-framed windows, its surrounding slopes dotted with holiday chalets clustered like chicks around a large mother hen, that they had reached journey's end.

Her knees were trembling when, immediately he drew to a halt, she stepped from the car.

'Please don't bother to get out!' She managed to keep her voice steady even though a tightness in her throat, a stinging behind her eyes, warned of tears that would both shock and embarrass him.

'I must see you settled in,' he insisted, easing his long legs on to the ground.

'Really, there's no need. Please don't delay any longer, Count Hugo, I suspect that you prolonged our journey deliberately, for my benefit, and I'm very grateful, but your mother must have been anticipating your arrival hours ago, you mustn't keep her waiting any longer.' Shyly, she extended a hand towards him. 'Thank you, again, for all the kindness you've shown me.'

He frowned down at his watch, then shrugged. 'I suppose you are right. Goodbye, Tarini, thank you for being such a pleasant and sympathetic companion.' Shock waves ran to the tips of her toes when he raised her hand to feather a gallant kiss across her fingertips. 'You never did give me permission to call you Tarini,' he scolded softly, 'however, it would please me very much to hear you address me less formally, even though my name must be coupled with goodbye.'

Willing him to go before the dam of heartbreak burst behind her eyes, she whispered painfully: 'Goodbye . . . Hugo . . . *auf Wiedersehen*!'

CHAPTER FIVE

Auf Wiedersehen! As Tarini sat musing, a solitary passenger on a chairlift which during the winter months was packed with skiers being transported to the topmost peaks, her poignant farewell to Count Hugo seemed whispered on the breeze teasing tendrils of hair against sun-kissed cheeks which already, in a mere couple of days, looked less hollowed, the shadows beneath her eyes almost dispersed by a strengthening glow of health.

Until we meet again! How inappropriate a farewell to a man who was destined to become a memory she would treasure for the remainder of her uneventful life. Count Hugo von Triesen, the man who, the proprietress of her hotel had proudly confided, was something of a national hero, a world-class skier upon whom ever Liechtensteiner had pinned his hopes of his country achieving an Olympic gold medal; an industrialist whose acute business acumen had brought increased prosperity to his tiny country; a man whose capacity for enjoyment was purported to be unlimited, whose name had been linked in the past with many of the world's most beautiful women yet who had somehow managed to avoid upsetting his ailing mother whose heart condition was so serious it was doubtful whether she could survive the shock of learning that so much as a breath of scandal had become associated with their ancient, honourable name.

News of his gallant behaviour towards the English maiden in distress who had somehow managed to miss her plane had circulated the hotel like wildfire, arousing the curiosity of fellow guests to such an extent that information happily doled out by the proprietress had merely whetted their appetites to the extent that Tarini had found herself being buttonholed time after time by individuals determined to hear her own personal account of the adventure, delving so persistently that eventually she had felt forced to seek escape in solitude.

'Grüss Gott, Fraülein!' As the elderly chair-lift attendant extended a horny hand, ready to pluck

her smartly out of the line of continuously moving chairs, she braced, then jumped the short distance to the ground before twirling breathlessly to watch her empty chair go speeding past on its return journey to the valley thousands of feet below. The old man laughed aloud, reading a look of proud achievement in blue eyes sparkling with excitement.

'*Grüss Gott*, Hans,' she beamed. 'At last I seem to be getting the hang of boarding and alighting while the chairs are still in motion. At least I didn't fall into your arms as I did the first few times I came up here.'

'Your performance is improving with every ascent, *Fraülein*,' he nodded, then, lips twitching beneath a heavily-drooping moustache, he teased gravely: 'Thanks be to God, I no longer need to dread the arrival of the young English *Fraülein* who catapults out of the chairlift and lands against my chest with the impact of a bolster stuffed with feathers!' Smiling his approval of the girl whose continuous appearances seemed to supply proof that she shared his delight in solitary walks among the mountain peaks, he questioned casually, so that she would not suspect that her movements were being anxiously monitored: 'Which path do you intend taking today, *Fraülein*? The weather is perfect, hardly a breeze, which is unusual at this height, nevertheless if you should walk too far you might overtax your strength.'

'I'll be careful, Hans,' she promised warmly, grateful for his concern, 'but in any case, I spend so many hours just sitting staring, bemused by the glorious scenery, that I don't spend half so much time walking as you appear to think. I love it up here,' she confided dreamily, 'the mountains are so rugged yet so steeped in peace, the silence falls heavily, and the air is so pure, flowing sharp as needles from a world of glaciers and eternal ice. Yet the meadows are golden with sunshine and vivid, heavenly-scented flowers spill out of every crack and crevice. God's very own rock garden,' she breathed blissfully.

'Yet one must always remember that the mountains' moods are variable, one minute darkly frowning, then blossoming overnight in the manner of a woman suddenly realising that she is loved,' Hans warned quietly.

Solemnly, Tarini returned the gaze of the old man proudly sporting the traditional Alpine outfit of knee-length socks and leather breeches supported by embroidered braces; white shirt worn under a sleeveless jacket decorated with two vertical rows of silver buttons; narrow-brimmed felt hat with a feathered cockade, who seemed endowed with wisdom gained from years of communing with nature, absorbing peace and tranquillity from his splendid surroundings.

Shyly, anxious not to give offence, she queried: 'Have you always worked on the chairlift, Hans?'

'Bless you, no!' His ruddy face was split by a wide grin. 'In my young days I was a ski instructor, at a time when the only way to ascend the snow-covered slopes was on foot and skiers had to stand sideways, using their poles as props, placing one ski obliquely in front of the other in order to ease their arduous way upwards. Often, to take our minds off the strain, we would compete to see who could trace the most geometrically perfect herringbone pattern on the frozen snow.'

'How exhausted you must have been by the time you reached the top!' she gasped, following the line of the peaks with eyes that had grown enormous. 'And what relief you must have felt on the downward run when all you had to do was let yourself go!'

Hans shook his head. 'Here in the Alps there are few great stretches of undulating country,' he corrected, 'only steep slopes, hairpin bends, and deep, precipitous drops, therefore the Alpine skier has to concentrate not so much on speed of descent as on the rapidity with which he can change course, come to a standstill, and on the length and daring of his flying leaps. Ah, the excitement,' he exclaimed, lifting yearning eyes towards the skyline, 'the sheer joy of rushing headlong down a slope, clearing a precipice by inches, veering swiftly in order to avoid large boulders and clumps of trees!' The fringe of his moustache was lifted by the blast of his regretful sigh. 'Sadly, those days are gone for ever, the only pastime left to me is woodcarving. I have a chalet in the mountains not far from here,' he hesitated as if uncertain of her reaction, then continued with gentle courtesy, 'some day, if you would care to and can spare the time, perhaps you might honour me with a visit, *Fraülein*?'

'I . . . I'd love to, thank you . . .' she stammered, taken completely by surprise. 'I can't tell you how often I've had to stop myself from peering through doorways and windows, how much I've longed to be allowed inside one of your fascinating Alpine houses.'

'Today, then?' The old man rubbed his hands together, looking as pleased as she felt. 'You usually finish your walk about lunchtime—if you are not expected back at your hotel, why not meet me here at noon and I'll take you home to share a bite with me?'

'Lovely!' Tarini accepted eagerly. 'I've told the proprietress of my hotel not to expect me back until early evening.'

'Then might I suggest that you take the lower path,' he pointed, 'which will lead you to the valley of gentians, a pleasant yet undemanding walk that should not leave you too tired to manage the incline leading up to my home.'

Buoyed with delighted anticipation, she almost skipped her way along the path Hans had indicated, feeling privileged by the invitation which she sensed was not extended to many, a kind gesture that had eased a little of the loneliness she felt even when surrounded by people of her own nationality.

Although the sun was beaming, snow was piled shoulder-high alongside paths which only weeks ago had formed *pistes* for swarms of eager skiers. Almost bursting with exhilaration and pure joy of living, she plunged her hands into its chilly depths to form a snowball, then, where rocks fell away disclosing a valley far below, she drew back her arm and flung the snowball with all her strength, chuckling delightedly as she watched it soar, then plummet downward until it vanished from sight.

'Carol won't believe me when I tell her about all this,' she murmured, smiling happily as she continued on her way, 'but then how does one find the words to convert a sceptic to the belief that crisp snow and hot sunshine can form a lasting relationship? How can one argue convincingly that although, in a matter of days, perhaps, the snow will have melted away like a guest who has overstayed his welcome, a marriage between contrasting elements can result in the creation of a paradise?'

When the path began dipping she knew she had almost reached the valley of gentians, yet in spite of its evocative name she was not prepared for the blaze of blue that erupted before her eyes. She blinked, shocked still by a vision of rare, heart-melting beauty. At her feet lay a meadow spread with an endless carpet of blue flowers standing head to head, densely packed, one against the other in joyful abundance. Almost robbed of breath, she dropped to her knees in the gentian meadow to examine more closely the tiny, stemless flowers lifting wide-open chalices of azure blue towards the morning sun. With a sigh of delight she sank lower until her body was resting supine, abandoned as a frail piece of flotsam on a blue velvet sea. Air filled with the scent of crushed petals; the lazy drone of a nearby bee, and the pointed turrets of Schloss Wolke just discernible against the skyline were the last things that registered before heavy eyelids dropped and she became transported into a land of dreams peopled with maidens in distress being plucked from danger by knights who arrived in the nick of time, not on dashing white chargers, but speeding, deeply crouched, on swishing skis . . .

'Miss Brown! Tarini!'

The voice sounded so much like Count Hugo's she smiled.

'Tarini, are you awake?'

Eyelids shot up over startled eyes when a note of impatience intruded into her dream. Dazedly, she tried to focus, fighting her way through a dream that refused to fade, unable to rid her vision of the blurred outline of features tanned heathen-dark by winter sunshine, eyes fathomless as the deep green depths of an Alpine lake.

'I'm sorry if I've disturbed your rest, but I must talk to you.'

Incredibly, the dream continued. Even though she was sitting up straight with her eyes wide open, and in full possession of her faculties, Count Hugo's profile remained superimposed upon a background of craggy peaks.

'What . . .?' She brushed a trembling hand across her eyes. 'Where am I . . .?' she pleaded on a gasped breath.

'In your valley of peace, I suspect,' he replied softly. 'No angel could look more blissfully contented had she stumbled into some long-lost paradise.'

'Count Hugo!' The realisation that she was awake, that the presence she had thought a mirage was in fact very human and looking wickedly amused, released a flood of embarrassed colour into her cheeks.

'What do you want? Why are you here? How

did you know where to find me . . .?' She jumped to her feet, bewilderment darkening her eyes to the deep azure blue of surrounding gentians.

'Hans pointed out the path you had taken. Please don't be angry with him, he seemed so pleased when I told him that we were friends. After enquiring at your hotel, I was advised to try taking the chairlift, as you had formed the habit of using it each day in order to spend time alone in the mountains. I must confess,' he frowned, 'that I found the knowledge that you spend hours walking in solitude slightly disturbing.'

'Why should any of my actions disturb you, Count Hugo?' she questioned stiffly, resenting the resurgence of emotions she had only recently managed to subdue, the erratic beating of a heart that had been reduced to calmness only after days spent repeating monotonously: *'Forget Count Hugo, you're unlikely to see him ever again!'*

'At the risk of sounding discourteous,' she choked, 'I must remind you that, although I'm grateful for the capable way in which you sorted out my affairs when I was in trouble, your responsibility was discharged the moment you deposited me outside my hotel. So, if conscience has forced you to seek me out, I can assure you the visit was unnecessary!'

He shrugged, and for a fleeting moment she suspected that he had been made to feel uncomfortable. Then immediately she dismissed the idea as impossible—no one looking as self-assured, as pantherishly relaxed in black, slim-line slacks and a matching rollnecked sweater, could possibly feel affected by her mild criticism.

But suddenly he surprised her with an uneasy, almost apologetic admission. 'My appearance was motivated by purely selfish reasons, I'm afraid. I have a problem, Tarini, and you are the only one who can help me solve it.'

Encouraged by the compassionate shadow his words had cast across her face, he reached for her hand and led her towards a large, conveniently placed boulder. 'Let's sit down,' he urged. 'I need time to consider how best to word my explanation.'

Obediently she waited, sitting quietly with her hands clasped loosely in her lap, wondering what lay behind signs of struggle chasing across his brooding profile.

'I'm afraid there's no easy way to soften the blow,' he finally decided, 'so I'm left with no option but to admit that I have been careless with a rather . . . er . . . incriminating piece of paper.' When his head jerked round to meet serene eyes clouded by a hint of puzzlement he frowned darkly, yet she was unprepared for the brutal spate of words that followed. 'Quite by accident—it doesn't matter how—the hotel bill for our overnight stay in Zürich fell into my mother's hands and, being the suspicious sort of person she is, always quick to jump to the worst possible conclusion, she immediately accused me of illicit behaviour and of using the name "Miss Brown" to hide the true identity of my companion who, as no doubt you can guess, she has assumed was Baroness Maria Frick, my fiancée. No amount of argument can convince her that she has assumed wrongly. Indeed, she has become so agitated over the imagined affair that her doctor has warned that unless she is calmed down immediately her health will be very gravely affected. Which brings me to the reason why I sought you out.'

Even in her state of numbed disbelief Tarini was able to recognise temper as the motive behind the tinge of colour running beneath his tan.

'I've tried to explain how the situation came about, step by step, detail by detail, but my mother still insists that Tarini Brown is a figment of my imagination, an alibi dreamt up to conceal my behaviour and to protect my fiancée's reputation. So you must see,' he leant forward in his eagerness,' how imperative it is that you two meet face to face—one look will be sufficient to convince her that she is mistaken, to make her realise how ridiculously unfounded . . .' He broke off, warned by her pinched, hurt expression that temper had loosened the reins on his tongue, resulting in her small amount of pride and self esteem being crushed beneath the weight of his stampeding words.

'Forgive me . . . I did not mean to give the impression——' Appalled by his lack of diplomacy, he lapsed into dismayed silence.

'Of course you didn't,' she agreed, managing to muster a few shreds of dignity. 'Naturally, you are upset, as is to be expected in the circumstances.'

'Then you will agree to help?'

When the proud Count Hugo von Triesen scoured her face with eyes unconsciously pleading she knew she could deny him nothing.

'It's the least I can do,' she told him simply, 'a small return for all the kindness you showed me when I was most in need of it.'

'Thank you, Tarini,' he heaved a sigh of relief. 'I felt certain I could count upon your co-operation. My plan may not work,' he shrugged, 'my mother, once her mind is made up, can be difficult to budge. However,' he attempted a belated compliment, 'I'm hoping that one look into your candid eyes, the sight of your patently honest face, will be sufficient to sway her stubborn attitude. Will you dine with us this evening?' he pressed swiftly, obviously anxious to arrange a definite time.

'If you wish,' she responded with outward serenity, praying he would not guess that the husk in her voice was caused by a throat tight within unshed tears. 'And please, try not to frown so,' she scolded, her gentle soul incensed by the selfishness of women who did not hesitate to put a man through torment in the name of love. 'It's my guess that the two women who matter most in your life are not incompatible but simply jealous of each other—the self-inflicted pain a woman feels when she realises that she has to share the love of a man to whom she is devoted. But sooner or later your mother must begin to accept the fact that jealousy is forgivable only on a young and beautiful face—just as your fiancée, if she's wise, must cease flirting with the risk of killing love and begin concentrating instead upon keeping it alive.'

She did not realise how vehemently partisan her words must have sounded until, after a moment's startled silence, he smiled, then with quizzical eyes fastened upon her troubled face, stated quietly, almost as if musing aloud.

'What a strange and very pleasant experience it is for me to have a female championing my cause. Past experience had taught me never to expect compassion from any member of a sex whose first principle is self-preservation. You're such a serious little soul, Tarini, yet you seem endowed with the power to make me look at the whole world with fresh eyes.'

She froze with fright when he leant close diminishing the gap between them. 'The meek shall inherit the earth,' he murmured whimsically, tilting her chin with one gentle finger. 'Heaven help us if that prophecy should ever come to pass, for I swear, caring heart, that you would not rest until you had given it all away.'

CHAPTER SIX

It had been a mistake, Tarini fretted, nervously pacing her bedroom waiting for eight o'clock to arrive, to have postponed her visit to Hans' home in order to ensure that she had plenty of time to get ready for the evening's ordeal. Count Hugo had escorted her back to her hotel and from the moment he had taken his leave she had wallowed in uncertainty, wondering what to wear, when to begin dressing for the dinner party and, most worrying of all, which attitude she should adopt towards the formidable Countess who had refused even to believe in her existence.

Pausing in front of a mirror to cast a despairing glance at newly-washed hair that hung even straighter than usual, with a plainness that lent to her face an impishness more suitable to a ten-year-old, she grimaced at her reflection. 'At least the Countess will be in no danger of suspecting that she's been brought face to face with a *femme fatale*,' she murmured. 'Count Hugo was right, my appearance will supply proof that I'm no mere alibi, and certainly no woman, however determined to believe the worst, could convince herself that a connoisseur of birds of brilliant plumage would choose to alight upon the nest of a nondescript English sparrow.'

The reflection that stared back at her seemed to amply confirm this theory—slight bird-boned figure trembling beneath a simple brown dress donned specifically to project an illusion of drabness, with a pleated organdie collar attached like a ruff, rising and falling over a pulse hammering in her throat. Timid blue eyes darted from a sight that was discouraging, and with quick nervous steps she moved away from the mirror and across to a window to gaze sightlessly into the darkness shrouding the majestic peaks she had quickly learned to love because up there she felt free, free to run; to laugh; to sing, to fling her arms wide and pretend to be flying, soaring higher and higher above a world in which she felt fettered by selfconsciousness, by lack of confidence, and by worry engendered by thoughts of a future empty of hope, happiness and love.

Exactly on the stroke of eight, a maid arrived to tell her that Count Hugo was awaiting her appearance in the foyer. As she had been ready for what seemed hours, all she had to do was shrug her arms into a short, collarless jacket as complementary to her dress as cream is to coffee, and to slip a small pochette bag over her wrist before making her way downstairs.

Thankful that her fellow guests were assembled in the dining-room anticipating their evening meal, Tarini hurried towards the foyer and saw Count Hugo waiting just inside the entrance.

'Oh . . .!' She halted at the sight of him, her heart feeling suddenly weighted. 'I didn't think . . . it never occurred to me . . .' she blushed, suffering an agony of embarrassment, 'that I would be expected to dress for dinner.'

The Count seemed to tower from a great height, his aristocratic bearing emphasised by a dinner jacket set easily as a cloak over broad shoulders, by a shirt contrasting crisp as snow against a darkly defined profile, by the discreet glint of diamonds linking the cuff around the hand he extended towards her.

'The style of your outfit is immaterial,' he frowned, seeming slightly on edge. 'In many instances I pander to my mother's whims because I feel it would be unfair to deprive her of some small victories,' he explained, placing a hand under her elbow to begin ushering her outside, 'however, her insistence upon clinging to outmoded practices need not concern you. Your appearance,' he flicked her a cool, green glance, 'is perfectly adequate.'

Had any girl ever received a more dampening tribute from her escort? she wondered miserably as once again she slid into the passenger seat of the car in which they had travelled from Zürich. He could have said she looked pleasant—even pretty should not have strained his credibility too far. But *adequate*. . . .! Yet honesty forced her to admit that so far as he was concerned sufficiency was probably enough, all he required was that she should be equal to the occasion.

As the car swept down the mountain road, gradually dipping, constantly twisting and turning, powerful headlights probed the undergrowth and picked out the contours of peaks lurking in darkness made black as pitch by heavy cloud obscuring the moon. Recalling a chance remark made by Hans, she relaxed and forced herself to make conversation.

'I believe we're not far from the Austrian border,' she began, just loud enough to penetrate his absorption.

'Wherever you may be in Liechtenstein you cannot be far away from either the German, Swiss, or Austrian borders, because our miniature country is a mere fraction over sixty square miles in area,' he told her so abruptly she felt like a child being rebuked.

Determined not to be browbeaten, Tarini continued doggedly: 'In that case, I suppose you know Austria well, must have visited it often?'

'Naturally,' he responded promptly. 'My fiancée, Baroness Frick, is Austrian, her home lies just across the border.'

'Oh, but ...' She began an objection, then thought better of it.

'Would you mind finishing what you were about to say?' Out of the corner of her eyes she saw his jaw tighten dangerously. 'You have a most infuriating habit of beginning a sentence and then hopping out of reach as if expecting it to explode in your face!'

Stung by the unjust criticism, she defended: 'I hesitated only because I was confused. I'm aware that, unlike my own country and yours, Austria has no monarchy, therefore, to an Austrian, a title would appear to be an anachronism.'

The look of resentment he tossed her way made plain his opinion that her words contained criticism of his fiancée.

'You and my mother should soon become friends,' he responded tightly. 'You appear to be two of a kind—both intolerant of minor vanities, ever ready to rip sharp claws through the fabric of human frailty.'

Tarini had imagined her small, hurt gasp was barely audible, yet the Count breathed an oath and swiftly drew the car to a standstill at the side of the road. Every nerve tightened when he snapped on the handbrake with a violence completely at variance with the friendly, almost fond rapport they had shared earlier that day.

'Women are the very devil!' he exploded, swinging his head round to direct a glacial stare. To Tarini's horror tears spurted into her eyes and began escaping beneath her lashes, chasing a silent course of misery down her pale cheeks. She sat very still, not daring to wipe them away, willing sharp, eagle eyes to be blind just this once to the distress signals of a victim who felt cornered, braced for the rip of sharp talons.

'I'm sorry, Tarini, please forgive me—the last thing I intended was to make you cry.'

His change of attitude took her by surprise. Slowly she lifted her head, wondering at the despair in his voice, at lines of utter weariness scored deeply into his face.

'I have no right to involve you in my affairs,' he continued dully, 'no right to use you as a whipping boy to relieve my frustrations.'

'Has something happened since we parted at lunchtime?' she enquired timidly, blue eyes soft with compassion.

Briefly, he nodded. 'Unfortunately, yes. Immediately I told my mother about your proposed visit she became extremely agitated—not because she felt any objection to meeting you,' he hastened to respond to her small cry of protest, 'but because, impatient fool that I am, I allowed her to guess my intention to leave for Austria first thing in the morning. When the doctor arrived he advised a mild sedative to enable her to sleep for a few hours and she agreed to take it only after it had been promised that she should be wakened in good time to receive you. However,' he sighed, 'once we left her bedroom her doctor issued a warning that for the next few weeks she must suffer no further upsets, must have complete rest and peace of mind, or else risk the gravest possible consequences.'

Tarini's heart somersaulted when, with a gesture of defeat, he raked his fingers through his hair, leaving it so tousled she was reminded of a bewildered, helpless boy.

'What am I to do, Tarini? Over yonder,' he nodded in the direction of the stretch of Alps dividing his country from neighbouring Austria, 'the girl I love is waiting, expecting my arrival in response to her decision. And over there,' he nodded in the opposite direction, 'lives a mother whose whims must be pampered if she is to live!' Suddenly he laughed, a harsh humourless sound that grated upon her nerves. 'I speak like a man who imagines he has a choice,' he jeered, glaring down as if he considered her solely responsible for his dilemma, 'yet how can I opt for a crown of love knowing that immediately it is donned I'll be crucified with guilt?'

When, with an impatient jerk, he switched on the ignition and set the car in motion Tarini knew that no reply was expected of her, that he would have been surprised, even annoyed, if she had ventured to offer an opinion, because she did not register upon him as a person, merely as a safety valve, an inanimate object to which he could confide his thoughts without fear of hearing them repeated. Her heart had no right to react with a pang each time he mentioned the woman he loved, the beautiful Baroness Frick who was so sure of his affections she had dared to adopt an impatient, foot-tapping attitude towards a proud man trained from birth to accept the burdens of duty. How certain she must be of his love, Tarini thought, suffering a pang of envy, sensing instinctively that the alluring Baroness was no gambler, that she would not risk throwing any dice that were not loaded in her favour.

As the car began ascending a mountain road leading up to Schloss Wolke, she forced herself to break his morose silence.

'I never cease to marvel at the industry and ingenuity of the Alpine race,' she confided pleasantly. 'Every peak has been made accessible even to novices such as myself by the erection of chairlifts, cable cars, and funicular railways. Before I arrived here, I imagined I'd have to be content with visual enjoyment, that the exhilaration of standing on the topmost peaks was a privilege reserved for fit, experienced climbers.'

'As once it used to be,' he responded, making an obvious effort to concentrate his mind upon her remarks. 'Were you disappointed by the discovery that the summits of most peaks are hives of industry, that where once you would have expected to find only eagles' eyries there are luxury hotels complete with indoor swimming pool, solarium, hairdressing salon, massage parlour, sun terraces and even conference rooms? That in place of huts built to shelter skiers and climbers in the event of a sudden snowstorm there are cafés and restaurants snuggled between slopes and perched within sight of each spectacular view?'

'Not disappointed,' she considered thoughtfully, 'but certainly surprised, and very grateful to the generous-natured locals who have made it possible for people such as myself to enjoy their magnificent environment. Surely you must resent us,' she queried softly, 'must often regret the invasion of noisy, gawking tourists into your peaceful solitude?'

She could tell by his slight hesitation in answering that she had delved deeply and touched a sore spot.

'For one so young, you are surprisingly perceptive—sensitive to the feelings of others,' he drawled laconically. 'Yes, you are right, there is a stone inside every cherry. But fortunately, progress has been confined to the foothills and when the pressures of society become too great those of us who consider privacy as necessary as food can escape to the inhospitable heights of the Jungfrau and the Eiger—a world of snowfields and ice towers, where a man can see his true self reflected in a mountain of glass.'

Before Tarini could tiptoe further into the mind of the man who sounded prison-pent, the outline of Schloss Wolke loomed in the car's headlights, an impressive pile of ancient stone set with a single malevolent eye of light leering from a lantern suspended from a chain hanging directly above huge, carved double entrance doors.

When she stepped out of the car and heard the far-off baying of hounds she shivered and drew the warmth of her jacket closer around her, wondering if the dogs had been left to roam and might suddenly bound out of the darkness mistaking her for an intruder.

'No need to look so apprehensive,' the Count chided drily, as he guided her to the top of a flight of stone steps, then strode to tug sharply upon an antiquated iron bellpull. Almost immediately the doors were opened by a manservant.

'Thank you, Josef,' the Count acknowledged the man's appearance with a nod. 'Please ensure that my mother is informed immediately that our guest has arrived.'

He drew Tarini forward and smiled slightly when, after advancing a couple of paces into the hall, she gasped and came to a sudden standstill. The hallway of Schloss Wolke was a revelation of grandeur undreamt of by the girl whose only previous knowledge of castles had been confined to short school trips around ancient piles left so long uninhabited they had finally been designated museums. Never before had she seen the starkness of antiquity softened, yet not marred, by the intrusion of modern comfort. Grey stone walls formed a perfect foil for huge Flemish tapestries, jewel-bright, so alive with detail she knew she could have sat entranced for hours deciphering legends recorded in fine silk and intricate needlework. Thick, luxurious carpet patterned in muted shades of grey, beige, and cinnamon brown flowed beneath sofas and armchairs offering the inducement of a plump, velvet-soft embrace. Massive carved chests and painted screens placed strategically in the path of any draught that might escape from the direction of doorways cut dome-shaped through solid stone were bathed in shadows cast by light beaming from the torch shaped globes of a chandelier suspended spider-fine from a vaulted ceiling.

Modern standard lamps glowed, highlighting the silken patina of low tables strewn with priceless bric-à-brac, and lending to the sculpted balustrade of a marble staircase a deceptive pink fragility.

Tarini's widely staring eyes blinked at a sign of movement at the head of the staircase, then blinked again, startled by a notion that some apparition from the past had begun a slow, dignified descent of the sweeping staircase.

'Mother!' She sagged with relief when Count Hugo's voice dispelled her fanciful notion. 'Are you certain you feel well enough to join us for dinner? If not, I'm sure, Tarini . . . Miss Brown . . .' he cast her an apologetic look across his shoulder as he began advancing towards his mother, 'will understand if you should decide to make your meeting brief.'

'Hugo!' Tiny, cameo features withered into a frown. 'Have you forgotten your manners? Kindly give me your arm,' she demanded, tapping the bottom step with the point of a silver-handled cane, 'and proceed to carry out a proper introduction!'

Though his expression did not change, Tarini sensed his air of resignation, read deep affection in the glance exchanged between mother and son. Tucking her hand into the crook of his arm, he began guiding the incredibly frail-looking old lady towards Tarini.

'Mother,' he flashed Tarini a green-eyed plea for tolerance, 'I'd like you to meet Miss Tarini Brown, the young English girl whose company I enjoyed during my flight to Zürich and whom afterwards, owing to unforeseen circumstances, I was privileged to escort to her hotel in Liechtenstein.

'Miss Brown,' gravely he inclined his head, 'my mother, the Dowager Countess Gina von Triesen.'

Fighting a strong impulse to curtsey, Tarini accepted the slender hand extended towards her and discovered it to be warm, its grip surprisingly friendly.

'I am delighted to actually meet you in the . . . er . . . flesh, as it were.' The Countess's smile cancelled out her critical appraisal of Tarini's too-slender figure, 'for I had begun to suspect that you were a mere mirage. Is this your first visit to our country, Miss Brown?'

Allowing her son to urge her in the direction of a sofa, she sat down and patted an adjacent cushion, inviting Tarini to join her.

Shyly Tarini obeyed, charmed yet overawed by the slight, regal figure wearing a dress with a black velvet bodice, its satin sleeves fringed and embroidered around the cuffs; buckled pumps peeping under the hem of a lavender satin skirt, and white hair crowned by a black velvet skull cap that had a face veil tossed back to form a misty black nimbus around delicate, patrician features. Undoubtedly, Tarini's romantic heart decided, the dowager Countess was a relic from a bygone age, an age of balls in summer palaces, of fur-upholstered sleighs pulled by prancing thoroughbreds, of banquets in halls with stone fireplaces huge enough to accommodate spit-irons on which whole oxen could be roasted.

'Well, Miss Brown . . .?' When the Countess's

gentle prompting made her aware that she had been staring, Tarini blushed and broke into an embarrassed flow of words.

'This is my first visit ever to a foreign country. I was ill for a while, and when my doctor insisted that I was in need of a holiday to build up my strength it seemed an ideal opportunity to fulfil a lifelong ambition to visit the Alps, and especially Liechtenstein, because everything I'd ever read about your country implied that it was unique in its atmosphere of olde-worlde charm.'

The Countess's expression managed to convey gratification and concern at one and the same time. 'You have been ill, you say? Then, my dear, you could not have made a better choice of location in which to recuperate. Not far from here is a shrine to which pilgrims have journeyed for centuries. Legend has it that a landslide, hundreds of years ago, demolished a prosperous but wicked town that formerly flourished in this area. Its inhabitants despised the teaching of the Church and had become pleasure-loving and self-indulgent. One day, an angel appeared to a woman of the town and urged her to go and pray at the chapel, so, leaving her child alone in the house with a bowl of porridge to keep it quiet, she obeyed the angel's command. But while she was kneeling in prayer she heard a terrible crash and a thunderous rumbling as if the end of the world had come. Horror-stricken, she rushed from the church and saw that the whole town had been destroyed—only her house was standing, and upon reaching home she found her child still quietly eating its porridge. You must ask

Hugo to take you to see the shrine that was erected to mark the incident, and which even today is the subject of tales of miraculous cures and of benefits that have never been denied a true supplicant.'

Tarini sensed rather than saw Count Hugo's frown. 'I'd love to visit the shrine if you could point out the way,' she hastened to ease his discomfiture. 'Count Hugo is a busy man, I wouldn't dream of encroaching upon his free time.'

'Nonsense, my dear,' the Countess exclaimed, 'you could not possibly find your way alone. My son gets bored with only myself and the servants for company,' the glance she exchanged with him was like the clashing of swords, 'your presence will keep him out of mischief, he shall take you to the shrine tomorrow morning.'

'Oh, but I couldn't possibly presume . . .' Tarini began, seeing Count Hugo's head jerk up in protest.

'Nonsense, I insist!' The Countess rose to her feet, silencing Tarini with an imperious wave. Two hectic spots of colour had appeared in her cheeks and as she faced them both, daring them to argue, her Dresden daintiness seemed to fade before their eyes. When she stretched out her arms towards Count Hugo appealing for his support, he strode to her side.

'What's wrong, aren't you feeling well?'

Bravely, she shook her head. 'Just a little weary, *liebchen*. I think, if your young friend will excuse me, I'd better return to my room.'

'But of course!' Tarini jumped to her feet, concerned about the old lady's over-bright eyes and trembling mouth. 'Please don't give me another thought.'

'Oh, but I shall think of you often,' the old Countess smiled, leaning heavily on her son's arm. 'Promise me, Hugo,' she coaxed, tapping his chest with the handle of her silver-headed cane, 'that you will take this child to the shrine tomorrow, then bring her back here for lunch? I must see more of the little candle whose light shines like a good deed in a naughty world.'

Tarini held her breath while he hesitated, knowing that his mind and heart were concentrated upon Maria, the beautiful baroness who was waiting expectantly for his arrival in Austria, whose attractions seemed to hold him even more powerfully than the bonds of duty.

Sensing his inner rebellion, the threat of overstretched loyalty about to snap, the Countess pleaded tearfully:

'Please, Hugo . . .!'

Reacting as if to the sting of a lash, his shoulders squared erect.

'Calm yourself, Mutti,' he intoned stonily, his profile bleak as storm-lashed mountain peaks. 'As ever, you shall have your wish.'

CHAPTER SEVEN

DRESSED in slim-legged denims, with a navy sweat-shirt pulled on over a pink and white checked blouse, Tarini was ready long before the time Count Hugo had arranged to pick her up at her hotel the following morning. Nervously she paced the forecourt, wishing she could think of some way of freeing him from his obligation to take her to see the shrine. She suspected, and so, she felt certain, did he, that the outing had been arranged by his mother solely to keep him from visiting Austria where, in the seclusion of Baroness Frick's home, he might be seduced away from all thoughts of duty in the arms of the woman he loved.

She was still fretting over the problem when he arrived in his car ten minutes later.

'*Grüss Gott*, *Fraülein*,' he greeted her gravely, startling her with the reminder that in spite of his perfect command of the English language, the apparent ease with which he commuted between his homeland and her own, he was actually a member of an alien race, one of those people whom her mother had been wont to designate 'unpredictable foreigners'.

'This morning,' he continued with a faint twinkle in his eyes, 'you remind me of an obedient little boy waiting scrubbed, tidied and neatly combed for the school bus.' Tarini struggled to force a smile on to lips that wanted to droop, trying not to dwell upon the thought that Baroness Frick would never find herself at the receiving end of such a back-handed compliment.

She was sitting beside him in the passenger seat, being driven away from the hotel, when she ventured to enquire: 'How is your mother today—feeling better, I hope?'

Immediately his face clouded. 'Unfortunately not. She spent such a disturbed night that I had to call once again upon the services of her doctor, who prescribed a sedative to ensure that she will sleep for the remainder of the day. In the circumstances, she will be unable to join us for lunch—I hope you don't mind?'

'Of course I don't!' she assured him quickly, then, as a thought crossed her mind, continued musing aloud. 'In which case . . .'

'You're doing it again, Miss Brown!' His dry note of censure sent her eyes slewing towards a profile set—as it all too often was—into tight lines of annoyance. He's like a grounded eagle, Tarini thought sadly, a freedom-loving creature made dangerous by his inability to soar, to sweep, and most imperative of all, to mate!

'Doing what?' she puzzled, just in time to prevent his impatience erupting.

'Exercising your infuriating habit of speaking just the beginning of a sentence, then leaving me to guess the remainder! Is your real world so unsatisfactory,' he jibed so cruelly she winced, 'that you have opted to live in a land of dreams, content to spend the rest of your life searching for a magic path leading to a mythical valley of peace?'

Striving hard to conceal her hurt, she tendered a quiet apology. 'I'm sorry. My mother also used to find my tendency to daydream a source of annoyance—"building castles in the air", she used to scold, before warning that many of my dreams might turn out to be nightmares if ever they managed to come true. In this instance, however,' she managed to sound much chirpier than she felt, 'far from daydreaming, I was following up a definite line of thought.' She drew in a steadying breath before daring to ask. 'How long does it take to drive to your fiancée's home?'

'A couple of hours,' he replied, obviously startled.

'In which case, it should be a simple matter to drive there and back in a day?' she continued thoughtfully.

'A very simple matter,' he frowned, 'I've done it often.'

'Then why not do it today?' she urged softly.

He braked so suddenly she was jolted forward, then back against her seat. Thankful that her safety belt was fastened, she tightened her grip on racing nerves and waited for his reaction.

Leaning forward, he glowered savagely. 'Was that remark inspired by spite, a devious female attempt to get your own back? I admit my manner has been less than courteous, that you have grounds for feeling peeved at the way you were hustled through dinner last night and then driven straight back to your hotel, but I felt certain that you would sympathise, would understand my agony of mind.

The very last thing I expected of you was malice. You know the circumstances as well as I do, so why do you torment me with such an impossible suggestion?'

'It's not impossible,' she countered shakily. 'On the contrary, what I proposed is extremely feasible. You're desperate to manage a meeting with your fiancée whose home is merely a couple of hours' drive away. Your mother seems set upon exercising every wile to prevent such a meeting, yet as you said yourself,' she reminded softly, 'she's unlikely to awake until evening.'

Dawning hope in his eyes twisted a double-edged knife in her heart, but after the first faint flicker it quickly died.

'I dare not risk it,' he rejected flatly. 'If by chance she should awaken before I return the outcome could be drastic.'

'But if I were to be there in your place,' Tarini insisted, 'I could tell her that you'd driven into Vaduz to attend to some small matter of business. The very fact that I'm there, supposedly awaiting your return, should prevent her from becoming suspicious.'

She blanched, but did not retreat from green eyes, raw with anticipation, raking across her face. 'Dear, honest Tarini,' he breathed, 'lover of truth, would you really be prepared to lie for my sake?'

'In this instance, yes,' she decided, praying that she would have no need. 'Even the devil has a right to justice . . .'

'Thank you, Tarini!' She wondered why his laughter sounded so stifled, then became incapable of thought when his lips descended, setting a seal upon his gratitude with a kiss that sent her senses soaring—higher than the turrets of Schloss Wolke, higher than dream castles built in the air; higher even than the spirits of a frustrated eagle to whom she had given the means of escape from his prison!

He left her installed in the garden at the rear of the castle, sitting in a chair placed on a terrace offering magnificent views of the mountains, with a tray holding coffee and biscuits at her elbow and a selection of books from the castle library to fall back upon in the unlikely event of her becoming bored during hours of enforced idleness.

For the first hour she was content to laze, soaking up sunshine, drinking in the sight of shaven lawns stretching without blemish before disappearing beneath a belt of surrounding trees. Then beds of geraniums daubed spots of brilliance so hurtful she closed her eyes until all that impinged upon her peace was the tinkle of water spouting into the basin of a marble fountain, a sound that gradually faded, growing fainter and fainter as she slid into a doze.

The sound of footsteps and the rattle of cutlery on an approaching trolley intruded into her slumber. She stirred, then opened her eyes, when a pleasant voice enquired:

'Would you like lunch served now, *Fraülein*?' She sat erect, pleasantly surprised to discover that she was hungry.

'Yes, please, Josef,' she smiled. 'But first I think I'd better peep inside the Countess's room to make certain she's still asleep.'

'No need, *Fraülein*,' Josef shook his head, 'my wife is keeping watch at her bedside, she will call you immediately the Countess shows signs of stirring.'

Completely reassured, Tarini helped herself from a mixed platter of charcuterie, fresh melon, cucumber, and tiny onions served with slices of crusty bread.

The fish that followed—swimming in butter sauce and spiked with almonds—was as much as she could manage, so regretfully she waved away Josef's offering of cream and chocolate gâteau.

'A cup of coffee would be lovely, Josef. If I eat any more meals as large as that one I'll get disgustingly fat!'

The very dignified manservant seemed to consider such an event so unlikely he smiled, then unbent far enough to joke:

'Miracles are not unheard of in this part of the world, *Fraülein*. Still, one should never risk overstraining the powers of the holy saints!'

Feeling blissfully contented, Tarini snuggled down in her chair to continue her nap, deliberately keeping her mind blank so that her day would not be spoiled by abortive fretting over Count Hugo and the decision he would have to make—a decision that would be made all the more difficult because whichever choice was eventually forced upon him, a loved one was bound to suffer.

She had just begun anticipating his return, to begin nurturing the almost certain assumption that his day-long absence was due to go unnoticed by his sleeping mother, when Josef appeared on the terrace. Immediately she saw the frown disturbing his normally impassive features she knew that he was aware—in the mysterious manner in which all family retainers seem to become aware of their employer's affairs—of the motive behind Graf Hugo's absence. The direction in which his sympathies lay was evident when regretfully he informed her:

'The Countess has awoken and is demanding to see her son, *Fraülein*.'

She jumped up, scattering a pile of magazines around her feet.

'What time is it?' she croaked, her colour high as a guilty conspirator's.

'Just seven o'clock,' he soothed. 'The Count has been away almost eight hours so, with luck, he should be arriving any moment now.'

Her slight figure stiffened, then with a dignity that brought a glint of admiration into Josef's eyes she took control of the situation.

'Then meanwhile, I'd better try to ensure that the Countess stays calm. Please ask Count Hugo to join me in his mother's room immediately he returns.'

A fretful question arose from the direction of a huge four-poster bed immediately Josef ushered her inside the Countess's bedroom.

'Are you certain my son has received my message? Go downstairs, Greta, and find out what is keeping him.'

The old lady's voice sounded slurred, and as Tarini stepped nearer the bed she was struck with pity for the tiny, shrivelled figure that looked swamped beneath a billowing, featherlight quilt.

'Are you feeling well enough to cope with a visitor, Countess?' She advanced, determinedly bright and smiling.

'Ah, the little *Schwächlinge!*' Dazed eyes struggling to focus upon Tarini's face seemed to confirm her suspicion that the Countess was confused, still under the influence of a powerful drug. Conscience stabbed heat into her cheeks when the old lady relaxed against her pillows, reacting exactly as planned. 'Come, sit by me, my dear.' A frail hand patted the side of the bed. 'I had begun to suspect that Hugo had deserted me, but as you are here, that obviously cannot be the case.'

Relieved that the extent of the Countess's confusion seemed confined to mere forgetfulness about her proper name, Tarini took the coward's way out and switched to a different subject.

'What a magnificent bedroom,' she murmured, sinking down into a chair at the side of the bed. 'I fear I should be too overawed to sleep in such surroundings.'

'I felt exactly the same way myself the first time I set foot inside this room—but then,' the old lady added with a surprisingly wicked twinkle, 'a bride should not expect to sleep much on her wedding night.'

Tarini's eyes widened as they roved the walls and ceiling of a room panelled entirely in wood, scrolled, carved and fluted, with wrought iron hinges stretching the full width of an enormous door; tapestry-draped windows; elaborately painted wardrobes and chests of drawers and, at the far end of the room, a Gothic black-lead tiled stove emitting waves of warmth towards the enormous bed. In spite of the warmth she shivered, imagining the reaction of a shy young bride to such majestic surroundings.

As if reading her thoughts, or perhaps reliving the feelings she had experienced during those first traumatic moments, the Countess sighed.

'To be the chosen bride of a Count von Triesen is an honour bestowed only upon women who have been proved worthy. While a man may feel tempted to ignore flaws evident in a mistress, protocol demands nothing short of perfection from the woman elected to be the mother of his sons.'

'Elected . . .?' Tarini's lips quirked with amusement. 'The word suggests that brides of previous Counts von Triesen were chosen by means of a vote.'

To her surprise, the Countess nodded, confirming a theory so outrageous Tarini had considered it a joke.

'A family has the right to veto any candidate it considers unsuitable for membership,' she stated proudly. 'I was one of many eager to become Countess von Triesen, but it was not until my background had been thoroughly investigated by my husband's family to ensure that my genes were suitable, that my bloodstock was acceptable, that my body was healthy and fertile enough to bear children, that my name was entered on to a short list from which my late husband finally chose a wife. Don't look so shocked, my dear,' the Countess seemed amused by blue eyes wide with disbelief, 'it is common practice among the European aristocracy for the bridegroom-to-be to take no personal part in the preliminary negotiations for a marriage. Invariably, these are left in the hands of family—and in such a way,' her voice suddenly hardened, 'many mistakes that might have been made by hotheaded young fools who considered their own selfish desires more important than purity of lineage have been prevented!'

Confronted for the very first time with a pride of heritage that verged on fanaticism, Tarini began dimly to recognise the enormity of Count Hugo's problem.

'Are you saying that there's no place in marriage for love?' she accused faintly.

'Love is a transitory emotion—marriage is for life, or should be.' The Countess's chin tilted. 'A pretty face is by no means the most important attribute of a wife. Every daughter of Eve is born with an instinctive knowledge of how to please a man, how to tempt a bridegroom into bed and satisfy his manhood to the extent that he ceases to dwell upon the fact that the union is one of convenience and eventually finds it an effort to recall the reason behind his initial uninterest. Most women make the mistake of relying too much upon good looks to hold a man's attention—the few who are wise concentrate upon developing the art of seduction.'

At the sight of Tarini's squirm the Countess broke into a weak chuckle. 'Have I embarrassed you, child? If so, I shall not apologise—feelings so rare and sensitive should be appreciated, not hidden like a rose wasting her scent upon a deserted garden. Intuition tells me,' she continued to display an iron core, 'that already you are a little in love with my son—don't bother to deny it,' she snapped when Tarini started violently. 'With such a fight on my hands I need the support of every available ally!'

Deciding that the pitiful old lady deserved to be humoured, Tarini reminded gently. 'Count Hugo has inherited your strong sense of duty, but also your iron will. The strain of being forced to reject one of the two women he loves best in life is bound to be intolerable. Surely the love you feel for him should enable you to accept a compromise?'

'Foolish girl!' The Countess heaved a hollow sigh. 'It is because his happiness is so important to me that I *cannot* compromise. Obviously he has confided in you—a happening I find remarkable—yet the impression you have formed of a selfish, possessive mother, jealous of her son's affections, is erroneous. I *want* my son to marry,' she insisted fiercely, her frail fingers plucking the cover of her bedquilt, 'but not to a woman who has already discarded two husbands!'

'Two?' Tarini faltered. 'Count Hugo mentioned only one.'

'Because Baroness Frick feels confident that her first mistake is too well buried in the past ever to be disinterred. I have indisputable evidence, however, that the first of her two marriages was contracted when she was barely seventeen years of age and dissolved less than a year later.'

'Why haven't you told Count Hugo?' Tarini gasped.

'And risk alienating him for ever?' Wearily the Countess shook her head. 'No, my dear, my son will respond to the demands of duty, honour and affection, but he will not bow to pressure. I dare not confront him with the knowledge that has come into my possession, for I am certain that the first one to provoke his temper will be the loser. My only hope is that in time he will come to his senses, that the affliction he calls love, which is actually no more than a temporary madness of the mind, will be cured completely. So you see, little *Schwächlinge*,' the old lady's eyelids closed as wearied by speech and anxiety she slipped once more towards oblivion, 'why you must help me to keep my son here in Liechtenstein. Between us we must try to discover an antidote that will cure him of his fever.'

Troubled by the very different slant that had been cast upon Count Hugo's affair with the beautiful baroness, Tarini left the old lady's bedside and wandered downstairs into the hall. She was slumped in an armchair facing the Flemish tapestry, wondering why all rescued heroines should be depicted as blonde godesses with voluptuous figures and long, slender legs, when she heard a door slam, then quick, impatient footsteps advancing in her direction.

Count Hugo's expression looked thunderous, bleak as the Eiger before the onset of a storm. Curling into a tight ball of nervousness, Tarini watched him stride across to a cabinet, where he poured out a drink, then tossed back the large measure of spirit in one gulp. Alarmed by his attitude of barely controlled violence, she forced herself to croak:

'What's wrong, has something dreadful happened?'

He swung round on his heel to face her then strode across the width of the carpet to tower over her cowering figure.

'*Damn you* for meddling in my affairs!' he charged thickly. 'Damn all of your sex—I swear that never again will I trust a woman, however long I may live!'

CHAPTER EIGHT

A WEEK had passed before Count Hugo's passions had simmered low enough to allow him to outline briefly the reason behind his savage outburst of anger.

Because his mother had insisted upon seeing Tarini every day—a five-minute visit that seemed to settle her mind and keep her happy and contented for hours—he had formed the habit of driving her from her hotel each morning to Castle Wolke, then, once her visit had been concluded, dropping her near whichever location she had decided to explore. He had never offered to accompany her, and even though his mother had often resurrected the subject, their proposed visit to the shrine had not materialised. Which was why, this morning, while he was driving her towards the funicular railway giving access to the mountains, she was startled by his dry, almost surly, offer.

'If you have nothing definite planned for today, I could take you to see the shrine of Saint Ludmila?'

'Thank you,' she accepted eagerly. 'The Countess has told me all about the shrine's magical properties, I should very much like to see it.'

His austere features darkened. 'My mother's mind is as rife with fanciful notions as your own,' he sneered, looking dangerously dark and smouldering. 'It puzzles me why the effects of her last attack should be lingering so long—if ever I were to discover that I was being deliberately manipulated . . .' he ground, leaving a threat hanging in the air.

'Oh, I'm sure you're not!' Tarini protested, distressed that such an unworthy suspicion should even have crossed his mind. 'Your mother's health is improving, she's growing stronger every day, yet there's no doubt that her latest attack has left her weak and in need of careful nursing.'

'You are probably right.' Much to her relief his jawline lost a fraction of its tension. 'If I am to be honest I must admit that the suspicion could have been born of wishful thinking.' Abruptly, he changed the subject. 'I see that you are dressed for walking,' he nodded approval of her neat brogues, checked blouse and serviceable jeans. He too was dressed in casual outdoor clothes—grey slacks and a matching roll-necked sweater—a choice of outfit that seemed to indicate that his invitation had been premeditated and not prompted by impulse as she had first imagined.

'We can go only part of the way by car,' he told her, 'then we must proceed on foot. The shrine is quite some distance from where I must park the car, but if you decide that you feel up to it, I'm certain you will find the walk rewarding.'

'Of course I feel up to it!' She could not help sounding slightly indignant. 'Each day since my arrival here, I've gradually lengthened the distance of my walks until now, after almost a fortnight of delicious food and sharp mountain air, I'm able to walk for hours without feeling the least bit exerted. *And* I've put on weight,' she boasted proudly, 'haven't you noticed?'

She wished the words unsaid immediately green eyes slewed in her direction. She squirmed, sensing hidden amusement in his slow, deliberate scrutiny of tanned cheeks devoid of hollows; blue eyes sparkling with newly-discovered vitality; a young, tender neck with a pulse leaping madly as her heartbeats; shoulders burdened only by the slightest of shrugs; the tilt of shapely breasts; a waist he could have spanned without exertion, and a trim length of calf and thigh saved from boyishness by a roundness that was unmistakably feminine.

She steeled herself to combat scorn, digging fingernails deep into her palms while she waited for the inevitable derogatory remark. But for once his lash was mild, the whip wielded by a less cutting hand.

'Your plumage may be far from exotic, little English sparrow, but your nut-brown daintiness has an appeal all its own. I wonder,' he tossed her amused glance, 'why I have never before noticed the enchanting army of freckles marching across the bridge of your nose?'

'They erupted only yesterday,' she told him stiffly, feeling threatened by a charm so lethal she considered it should have been subjected to control by licence. 'I must keep a look-out for a chemist's shop, there's a cream on the market which supposedly encourages them to fade.'

'Why bother?' he drawled unkindly. 'Faultless beauty is an attribute not given to many. However, you may find consolation in the knowledge that our local woodcarvers discovered long ago that it is small imperfections that make hand-made objects most desirable.'

As he drove higher into the mountains she lapsed into hurt silence, deflated by the comparison she felt had reduced her to the level of a piece of paste daring to aspire to the perfection of a flawless gem. And yet, she had to admit, with the image of his lovely fiancée to use as a criterion, how could he consider her otherwise? Against Baroness Frick, she must appear pallid as a shadow is to substance; colourless as a faded print compared with the vivacity of its original subject.

Yet by the time they had reached the summit of a winding road rising thousands of feet above lowland made lush by the meandering Rhine, her spirits were revived, as always, by the sight of a stream tumbling from glacial peaks; by grazing, doe-eyed cattle, and by the miniature Alpine huts in which herdsmen remained during the entire summer, tending the cattle, keeping a careful record of the yield of rich yellow cheese and creamy butter provided by each animal.

Sharing a tacit belief that speech would be an intrusion into their majestic surroundings, they walked in companionable silence, drinking in beauty intoxicating as wine, breathing air sparkling, fresh and golden as champagne bursting bubble-bright from forest-green depths. Apparently feeling no need of words, the Count took her hand as they began approaching the mouth of a tunnel gouged out of granite, and carefully ensured her safety as they negotiated the dark recesses of a tunnel running a quarter of a mile through solid rock to give access to a hidden, enchanted valley.

She blinked when they emerged into sunlight and stood rapt, listening to the voice of nature reminding her of days not long past when the superstitious mountain people still believed in miracles and magical creatures that were said to have inhabited the glens, ravines and dark forests; in witches, elves and kobolds; good and evil fairies, and saints that had descended in human form to answer the prayers of the needy and to punish the ill-doers. She was so wrapped in fantasy that Count Hugo had to speak twice before his voice registered.

'Waken up, child!' he unbent far enough to tease. 'You look as if you are expecting the arrival of a scaly dragon belching fire from his nostrils in the manner of all the best fairy tales. These days, it is impossible for any would-be hero to find a maiden waiting to be rescued—unless,' he laughed unpleasantly, 'one has a mind to place a stranded air traveller in that category.'

Tarini sighed, hating the supercilious overtone threatening to spoil her first glimpse of a secret valley tucked away behind a granite screen of mountain, a quiet, protected pasturage with a rich yellow carpet of flowers that transformed a shaded spot, buried all winter under ice and snow, into a private paradise.

'What a heavenly place! And such flowers . . . I don't believe I've ever seen this variety before!'

'They are called *Mutterkraut*—Mother's weed—by herdsmen who are invariably on the look-out for the yellow-flowered, broad-leafed plant they believe increases the flow of cows' milk.'

They walked on, then came without warning upon the shrine of Saint Ludmila set in a niche cut into rock on the far bank of a stream, a weather-worn but still sweet-faced figure wearing a milk-maid's dress, with golden rays of sunshine forming a halo around her head. Peering more closely at the statue, her breath reverently held, Tarini whispered:

'I can't quite make out what she's holding.'

'A harvesting sickle in one hand and a milk jug in the other,' he supplied, 'as befitting the patron saint of dairymen, herdsmen, milkers, butter separators and cheese makers. Also, Alpine cattle are reputed to come under her special protection. If you look closely, you can just distinguish at her feet the whitened skull of what must once have been the *Schwächlinge*, which translated means, "the weakling", a small cow built up by legend into a worker of miracles.'

'Little weakling!' The old Countess's peculiar form of address echoed in Tarini's ears, bringing with it a reminder of how insistent the old lady had been—how fretfully anxious—that Count Hugo should accompany her on a visit to the shrine. Feeling inexplicably cold all over, she dropped down on her knees and patted the grassy space beside her, inviting as calmly as she was able:

'Why not sit down and tell me all about the little weakling?'

Sunshine lent to his hair the sheen of sable as he stretched out full length upon the grassy back with a stalk of grass clenched between his teeth. Shading his eyes from the sun, he chewed thoughtfully, as if having to dredge his memory for items of folklore gleaned during childhood.

'The "little weakling" was supposedly a lady whose lack of good looks was far outweighed by burning ambition. Do you recall my mentioning the "queen cow" and the attributes needed to acquire such a title?'

She nodded. 'She had to be nominated best cow of the herd, highest in yield of milk, cheese and butter.'

'And usually, the most good-looking,' he confirmed, 'a sturdy Alpine beauty capable of spouting milk in great warm, frothy streams, blessed with a fawn satin coat, huge gentle eyes and the long curling lashes of a beauty queen. In short, a lady with presence, one not likely to be overawed by her position of leader of the procession.'

'The procession . . .?' she queried. 'The one in which the champion of champions leads the herd with an upturned milking stool fixed between her horns?'

'So you don't dream all of the time, little sparrow,' he tilted, slightly jeering, 'you do listen to some of the things I say?'

'Always,' she stammered, confused when he suddenly shot upright, hovering like a bird of prey. Resorting to cowardice, she turned her head aside, then, anxious for him to continue, she murmured, 'Were you about to tell me that it was the weakling's ambition to be queen of the herd? Not for her own sake, I'm certain, but probably for the sake of a loved one.'

'You have heard the story before,' he stated flatly, sounding slightly disappointed.

'No,' she shook her head, 'I don't need to be told about the sacrifices females are prepared to make in order to ensure the happiness of those they love.'

His short laugh echoed with all the bitter anger she had sensed simmering inside of him since his return from his fiancée's home. 'Forgive me if I sound cynical,' he paused to touch the flame of his lighter to the tip of a cheroot, 'but at the risk of destroying your romantic ideals, I must argue that most females—present company excepted, of course,' he forced out the gallantry, 'seem prepared to squeeze a man dry of emotion, then toss his husk to the four winds.'

Tarini kept her eyes fixed upon distant peaks, conscious that he was glowering, brooding darkly upon the visit to Austria that she had urged him to take and its disastrous outcome for which, unreasonably, he seemed to hold her solely responsible. Desperate to understand why the Countess should have concluded that the story of the little weakling ran in some way parallel to her own, she dared to intrude into his melancholy mood.

'Does the legend have a happy ending?'

'I'm sorry . . .?' She chanced a sideways glance and saw that his eyes had a dazed, faraway look, the look of a man jerked back from the brink of some unfathomable chasm. 'Oh, yes, the legend!' With an obvious effort he abandoned thoughts of the past in order to concentrate upon the present. 'How far did I get?'

'Not far,' she managed to smile, 'you were side-tracked almost at the beginning when you were about to tell me about the procession.'

Something about her unhappy eyes, a mouth drooping despondent as a child's, must have stirred his conscience, for he surprised her by cupping a hand beneath her chin, tipping it high until she was forced to meet eyes warming slowly as an Alpine lake melts the ice-green crust of winter.

'Don't fret, Tarini,' the edges of his mouth frayed into humour, 'you shall not be deprived of your fairy tale.' Terrified by the effect of his cool touch upon her skin, she jerked her blush-hot face out of reach and settled down to listen.

'Each autumn when the first threat of snow comes to the high passes, peasants come from miles around to gather at the mouth of the tunnel we have just passed through to cheer and wave to the herdsmen returning cows to the lower pastures, pushing and shoving to acquire the best vantage points as they wait for the deep hollow booming resounding from the black metal bell hung around the neck of the "queen cow" chosen to lead the procession. Deafening cheers indicate the first sighting of the queen who invariably plays up to her position by hesitating when she emerges into the light and standing like an actress on stage acknowledging the applause of her audience. As well as a huge bell fitted with a silver clapper and a milking stool perched on her head like a beribboned Easter bonnet, she wears a coronet of laurel leaves, bunches of meadow flowers tucked inside her leather collar, and a crimson heart on her forehead—the most coveted symbol of superiority.

'The procession winds down the mountainside in order of rank—the champion, the next best, the winners of minor rosettes, then decorated horses drawing carts piled high with fat tubs of butter and yellow cannonball cheeses. Then lastly, the saddest sight I have ever seen, animals whose milk production could only be classed as average, their unhappy expressions providing proof for anyone who needs it, that four-legged beasts are capable of emotional feelings. As you have probably guessed, the little weakling was always one of the last to emerge from the tunnel—thin-flanked, sad-eyed, and dejected, very conscious of her inability to bring a coveted prize to her poor-peasant owner.'

Tears raced unchecked down Tarini's cheeks because to have attempted to wipe them away would have been to invite some caustic remark from a man who had little patience to spare for over-emotional females. She stared fixedly ahead, hoping to avoid exposure, and was horrified when his hand hove into view, positioned directly in the path of a huge tear ready any second to plop from the edge of her chin.

When it eventually did, he reacted exactly as she had feared.

'What the . . .!'

Hastily, she mopped up surplus tears with a tissue before turning a shamed face towards him.

'You're not—you *can't* be crying!'

'I . . . I'm afraid so,' she laughed shakily, then dug her teeth into a quivering bottom lip, praying that he would not be too unkind.

Saint Ludmila must have interceded on her behalf. Instead of sounding exasperated his response was amazingly tender.

'You are a very warm, caring person, Tarini.' Turning her woebegone face to the sun, he dabbed at the residue of tears with a crisp, man-sized handkerchief until he was satisfied that the reservoir of compassion had been dammed, then scolded gently: 'You are far too vulnerable, little sparrow, there's heartbreak enough to be found in day-to-day living without expending your emotions upon a fictitious character bearing no relation to real life.'

She wanted to choke out a denial, to tell him how completely she could identify with the little weakling who had yearned to be transformed from a drab nonentity into a vision of loveliness that might attract everyone's attention—not that she wanted everyone's attention, just the attention of one particular man who seemed blind to the fact that she was a woman, who scolded her as if she were a child, and confided his troubles only because he was confident that she was no more than a stranger soon to pass out of his life. A man who would react with embarrassed astonishment if ever he were to discover how completely she had fallen in love with him!

Becoming conscious of a quizzical gaze which, given sufficient time, might be capable of reading secrets tucked inside the thickest of pages, she made an effort to distract his thoughts away from herself.

'Tell me,' she gulped, 'did the little weakling ever realise her ambition?'

'Ah, now that is the point where Saint Ludmila comes into the story!' To her enormous relief he rose quickly as a perch to her bait, yet she sensed in his voice a hint of impatience, the boredom of a man with scant sympathy to spare for the dull and mediocre. 'Having been reared upon tales of miracles brought about through praying at the shrine of the saint, the young daughter of the little weakling's owner, knowing how much her family's prosperity depended upon the yield of their one and only cow, decided to take matters into her own hands. To cut a long story short,' a quick glance at his watch seemed to confirm his growing impatience, 'she separated the little cow from the rest of the herd and brought her here to the valley where she was left to graze while the child spent hours praying to Saint Ludmila. At milking time that same evening the herdsman was astonished when, in place of the thin, bluish trickle of milk fit only for feeding to pigs, a warm, rich, creamy jet shot into the milking pail placed beneath the little weakling. Soon the pail was filled to overflowing and another one was put in its place. It too was filled with foaming milk, and three hours later the miracle was repeated. By the end of that week she had caught up and surpassed the best of her herd and won for herself the honour of wearing the milking stool between her horns when she led the procession during the descent to the valley the following day.

'Outside the tunnel, an even bigger crowd than usual had gathered to witness the appearance of the weak creature who had blossomed into a heart-warming beauty. People cheered themselves hoarse when they saw her washed, brushed, with her pale hide glistening, hooves and horns sparkling in the sunlight, as she stood poised in all her regalia at the mouth of the tunnel. She carried out her duties with the aplomb of a beauty queen, but later that evening the efforts of the previous week began to tell and, worn out by her efforts, the little weakling died before sunrise the following day.'

Casually, he rose to his feet and began brushing pieces of grass from his clothing. 'There now, that has disposed of the little weakling—let us hope, for ever!'

Distressed by his rough handling of her ragged emotions, Tarini jumped to her feet and moved quickly away, prevented by the lump in her throat from expressing her disgust of his callous attitude.

'One moment, Tarini!' Sharply, he commanded her attention. 'I did not bring you here merely to recount a fanciful legend, there is a matter of importance I wish to discuss.'

She hesitated, then with her back still turned, mumbled: 'What is it you want?'

'When are you due to return home?' The question took her by surprise. Slowly she turned round to face him. 'The day after tomorrow—why?'

He hesitated, then with a shrug continued baldly: 'You told me that once you arrive home you'll have to begin searching for employment. You've also mentioned how much you have enjoyed your visit to my country, how much your health has improved during your stay in the mountains. Your remarks led me to wonder whether you would consider staying on in Liechtenstein, to accept the position of companion to my mother? Your duties would be light, of course,' he assured her swiftly, 'merely seeing to it that she is kept amused, is made to rest when she should, and has a compatible companion during her leisure hours.'

She stared, wondering if she had heard him aright, if she really *was* being offered the heaven-sent opportunity of staying a while longer in the country she had learned to love, of living in the home of the man she loved! Then realisation dawned. In a tone as heavy as her heart, she intoned:

'Am I to assume from your request that you and Baroness Frick intend to marry?'

'No, we do not!' he rapped. 'Thanks to your

meddling, that event is no longer likely to come about.'

'My meddling . . .?' she gasped, unable to conclude the astonishing accusation.

As if made uncomfortable by her look of amazement he swung away. 'I'm sorry,' he jerked across his shoulder, 'that was probably unjust. No doubt your intentions were good when you urged me to visit Austria to make my peace with Maria. You were not to know that when I arrived at her home I would find her determined to return my ring unless I agreed to settle upon a definite date for our wedding.'

'Oh, I'm so sorry!' A sob rose straight from her heart, a heart that was no stranger to the anguish of rejection.

'Don't be,' he snarled, pride rearing against the humiliation of being pitied. 'I've been taught a salutary lesson—never again will I allow myself to be contaminated with the mad malaise commonly known as love. Don't look so shocked,' he tossed her a grim, humourless smile, 'far from developing into a woman-hater, I shall continue enjoying the company of your fair sex. But on my terms,' his lips set into a thin dangerous line, 'and those terms shall exclude me from any degree of commitment! However,' he swung round so quickly she jerked backward, wanting to flee as far as possible from the tense, aloof figure seething with inner anger, 'I still have a need for freedom—will you take the job I have offered, Tarini, will you promise to stay with my mother and so make it possible for me to discard some of the chains of duty?'

Giving no thought to the hurt she was bound to encounter in the future, wanting only to minister salve to his lacerated pride, she stammered out the promise:

'Of . . . of course, I'll stay, if you want me to—if I'm allowed to. But will I be able to obtain a work permit?'

Like a shadow passing across the sun, a curtain drawn suddenly over a lighted window, his expression closed down before her eyes.

'Liechtenstein's laws regarding the employment of aliens are extremely strict. Foreigners are allowed to work here for only a very short time before being forced to leave the country.'

'Then there's no way that I can help!' she choked, wondering why, in the circumstances, he had bothered to raise the suggestion in the first place.

'Oh, but there is a way.' She could barely make out sibilant words hissed between lips set stern as stone. 'You are the only girl of my acquaintance who does not have an exaggerated opinion of her own worth,' the merciless voice continued, 'the only one I would trust never to exploit a delicate situation, never to expect more than she has been promised. In short, Tarini, you are the only female I would consider taking as a wife, the only one I would trust to uphold the high moral standards expected of a Countess von Triesen!'

CHAPTER NINE

THE delicate state of the Countess's health offered an acceptable excuse for making the wedding a quiet, informal affair to which the minimum of guests had been invited. Even Carol was not able to be present. Laid low at the very last minute by a particular virulent attack of influenza, she had telephoned Tarini and in a husky, unfamiliar voice had apologised through tearful coughs and sneezes.

'I'm so worried about you, Tarini,' she had croaked. 'When I read your letter telling me that you wouldn't be returning home just yet as you'd decided to marry some foreign Count I was absolutely knocked out. And now I can't even come to discover for myself whether you've been bewitched or are merely besotted! Are you sure you're doing the sensible thing, my pet?' Her worried question had been projected on a note of high hysteria. 'Can't you wait just a little while longer before committing yourself to marriage with a man you met in the airport less than a month ago?'

If they had been face to face Tarini would probably have admitted the true state of affairs, but finding it impossible to confide her hopes and fears into an impersonal mouthpiece, she had fallen back upon the reassurance:

'I'm being extremely sensible, Carol, so please stop worrying about me and concentrate upon getting well so that you can come and see for yourself what a very fortunate girl I am.'

A pause had fallen upon the crackling line before Carol had responded soberly: 'You sound as if you're very much in love, Tarini. If that's the case, then all I can say is congratulations to you both and may you reap all the happiness you deserve. I once read somewhere that marriage can make people pleasanter, kindier, more understanding and easier to get on with—I hope your bridegroom appreciates the fact that, in your case, that would be impossible, for not even marriage could make you a nicer person than you were before. I'm broken-hearted at the thought of you walking down the aisle less than an hour from now without a friend to support you on your great day—but don't feel deserted, Tarini, I promise I'll be with you in thought every inch of the way.'

Dejectedly, Tarini had replaced the telephone receiver on its rest, feeling an aching need of her friend's comforting presence, yet at the same time feeling slightly relieved that Carol's too-perceptive eyes would not be probing Hugo's face, wondering why a man about to embark upon marriage should be displaying the sort of blank indifference that had been evident in his manner during the two weeks that had elapsed since his startling proposal.

Even now that it was time for her to begin dressing for the ceremony she could hardly believe that she, plain, nondescript Tarini Brown, was destined to become the next Countess von Triesen!

Sheering away from the reminder that their wedding certificate was to be no more than a contract between employer and employee, she slid out of her dressing gown and into the plain silk slip that formed the basis of the wedding gown the Countess had insisted upon buying.

'It shall be part of my wedding gift to the bride.' To forestall further argument she had beaten a rapid tattoo with her stick upon the stone-flagged floor of the terrace. 'Once you are married, it will be my son's privilege to provide a suitable wardrobe for his wife, but not your wedding dress—such a purchase would not be *comme il faut*.'

Instructions had been sent to several high-class shops in the tiny capital of Vaduz that the Countess wanted some of the finest samples of bridal wear sent to Wolke Castle, and the offerings, once they arrived, had been so breathtaking that Tarini had been faced with an almost impossible decision.

She was posing in front of a mirror, wearing the dream dress she had finally chosen, when a knock sent her spinning round to face the door.

'May I come in, *Liebling*?' Anticipating a welcome, the Countess advanced slowly into the room and sank down on to a chair, keeping her eyes fixed upon Tarini's slender, white-gowned figure.

'A perfect choice for a quiet, simple ceremony,' she nodded, smiling approval of the French embroidered voile floating cloud-soft, lending fullness to tender young curves, adding an extra depth of purity to a sweet face innocent of make-up, yet made radiant by eyes reflecting the deep velvet blue of tender, easily-crushed gentians that flowered best tucked away in secret, solitary places.

'You have excellent taste, my dear,' the Countess

decided. 'That slim band of ribbon holding one perfect white blossom against your brow, and the charming frilled parasol, make a perfect substitute for the traditional wreath and veil. And now for the finishing touch!' Grey taffeta rustled as she searched the folds of her skirt for a pocket from which she withdrew a small leather jewel box. 'Open it!' she urged, holding the box towards her, 'I'd like you to wear this during the marriage ceremony.'

With slightly trembling fingers Tarini pressed a catch to release the lid, then shrank from the sight of a heartshaped ruby contrasting blood red against a cushion of white velvet. She stared, feeling pained as if it were her own heart dragged out of her body, wondering at the old lady's stubborn refusal to acknowledge the true reason behind their marriage; her insensitive insistence upon continuing a charade born during her delirium which seemed to have developed into an obsession.

Swallowing hard to disperse a hurtful lump in her throat, she scolded as steadily as she was able: 'I know you mean well, Countess, but you really must try to dismiss the notion that I'm a reincarnation of the little weakling, the miracle worker who succeeded in routing all opposition and took pride of place at the head of the procession wearing a crimson heart as an emblem of victory. I cannot accept such a costly gift under false pretences—you know why your son proposed to me,' she accused sadly. 'He's not in love with me, but because he has become embittered with life, determined never to allow himself to fall in love again, he is prepared to enter into a marriage of convenience for your sake, because he thinks I can be of help to you, and because marriage is the only way round laws which make it impossible for me to reside here indefinitely.'

'Don't be such a defeatist!' The Countess glared at the girl standing with head drooped, wilting as a snowdrop in summer heat. 'Sceptics also implied that the little weakling owed her change of fortune more to the munching of the beneficial *Mutterkraut* than to the intercession of Saint Ludmila! Prayers are not always answered in a straightforward, understandable way yet what does it matter so long as the object is achieved? I have prayed long and hard to the blessed Ludmila that my son might be saved the consequences of his own folly and in a very short time, when Hugo's ring slides upon your finger and you are declared the new Countess von Triesen I shall rest content, confident that my prayers have been answered. After that, the outcome will be entirely up to you. After all, if you intend to marry for ever what can possibly go wrong? All you need do is make yourself indispensable by sharing in his affection and desires, by sharing his home, his bed, and eventually, I hope, sharing in the creation and care of a family. If you make certain, *Liebling*, that every slight overture of friendship is gratefully received and warmly returned you will eventually reap the satisfaction of finding him more and more reluctant to absent himself from a warm, loving atmosphere far more satisfying than any transitory sensations he might find in the arms of the "other woman".'

Though she did not refer to her by name, Tarini sensed that the Countess's mind was on Baroness Frick, the woman whose beautiful shadow seemed destined to be cast forever over the occupants of Wolke Castle.

'Now put on the pendant,' the Countess ordered, rising to her feet, 'it is almost time for you to leave for the church. When you walk down the aisle remember to hold your head high, as befits your new position.'

Speared into action by a commanding look, Tarini lifted the jewel from its velvet bed and fastened the clasp of the chain around her neck so that the heart nestled between the curve of her breasts. pulsating in time with her heartbeats. Hesitantly, she turned, her eyes filled with gentle pleading and an infinite longing to be loved as she waited for the old lady's approval.

'Dear Saint Ludmila,' the Countess murmured, 'give her the sweetness and warmth of your protection!' Then she opened her arms wide, tilting her cheek to invite a kiss. 'Go now, my dear,' she breathed against Tarini's cool, faintly-scented cheek, 'and always bear in mind that the love of a sincere and tender heart has been known to alter stars from their courses!'

All the servants were assembled in the hall when she and the Countess arrived downstairs, and to her delight she saw that they were wearing beautiful traditional costumes rarely seen except on festive occasions, the girls looking especially lovely in gaily embroidered blouses, bodices and skirts, each wearing a cap made of intricate, handworked lace.

Hans, his Sunday-best suit smartly pressed and with silver buttons shining, stepped forward to greet her. Clicking his heels smartly, he bowed first to the Countess and then to Tarini, staring misty-eyed, almost, she thought, as if he was entranced by some rare and beautiful sight so unconnected with herself that she reacted with surprised confusion to the old gallant's greeting.

'God giveth all things to enjoy—the sunset and the rainbow and the rose. Yet nothing in my memory can compare with the sweetness, grace and blushes of a lovely young bride.'

Tongue-tied with shyness, Tarini could do no more than acknowledge the old man's compliment with a smile. The Countess, however, was not lost for words.

'That silver tongue has not rusted with age, you old rascal!' Though she tapped her stick against the floor, her lips were twitching. 'I shudder to think how many girls of my generation were taken in by the flattery of a handsome young skier whose speed of descent could only be equalled by the rapidity of his wooing.'

Hans shrugged. 'Men being men, and women being women, we must all try our hands at courting, Countess.' His twinkling eyes exchanged a look of regard with the old lady who seemed to know him so well. 'But there was method behind our flirting because, like the little English bride, when we eventually decided to marry we chose wisely and well.' Then he drew himself tall and with a look of immense dignity addressed the smiling assembly of servants.

'As you are all aware, the future Countess von Triesen has done me the great honour of asking me to carry out the duties normally assigned to the father of the bride. Therefore, it is in that capacity that I urge you to set off without further delay and take your places in the church so that Count Hugo—never the most patient of men—may be spared the strain of a prolonged wait for the appearance of his bride.'

The excited, laughing servants were crowding around the door, pushing and jostling as they teased the young man at the front who was having difficulty manipulating the heavy iron ring attached to a latch fashioned centuries ago to withstand pressure exerted by any unwelcome foe, when the door bell clanged so loudly and suddenly they were all shocked into silence. Josef, mindful of his position, waved them aside and in his usual dignified manner flung open one half of the massive door.

Immediately the uninvited guest stepped over the threshold Tarini sensed that she was looking at Baroness Frick, the legendary beauty whose petulant demands had caused Hugo so much torment.

'Forgive me, Countess, if I have called at an inconvenient time, but I've such an urgent need to talk to Hugo that I've driven non-stop since leaving home early this morning.'

As the Baroness glided rather than walked towards the old lady standing ramrod-straight, shocked eyes glaring out of a pale face set stiff as parchment, Tarini's wide eyes drank their fill of the elegant, graceful girl dressed entirely in silver grey, a fine woollen suit—which must, she thought, have cost more than nearly all the items packed into her own shabby suitcase—fitting glove-smooth around full, rounded breasts; incurving waist, and tapering thighs of the tall, Alpine beauty. Hair the colour of ripe corn, parted severely, then swept in satin wings towards a chignon coiled low on the nape of a slender neck, lent emphasis to a patrician profile, to a storm-grey eyes framed with dramatically darkened brows and lashes, and to a pink, pouting mouth that seemed to tighten while she waited for the Gräfin to recover her equilibrium sufficiently to enable her to disperse the heavy fall of silence.

Though the inopportune appearance of her son's ex-fiancée threatened the realisation of her dearest hopes, the old lady managed a superb recovery.

'You must excuse my lack of courtesy, Baroness; our household is disorganised because of a wedding due to take place less than fifteen minutes from now. The servants were just about to leave for the church when you rang the doorbell—would you excuse me a moment while I speed them on their way? And the little bride, too, of course, for she is so eaten up with wedding nerves she's quite likely to be tempted to back out of the promises made to her waiting bridegroom unless she is despatched to his side without delay!'

Tarini gasped, realising that, without a flicker of shame, the Countess had delegated her to the position of a humble servant overwhelmed by the honour of being allowed to use the facilities of her employer's home on her wedding day.

Uninterested grey eyes swept over the quivering ashen-faced bride, then returned quickly to the old Countess. 'By all means do all that you have to do, Countess,' the completely duped Baroness murmured, 'one must never opt out of responsibilities owing to those who look after our comfort, however tedious or inconvenient they might sometimes become.'

'Thank you so much,' the old lady responded with an ironic acidity that only Tarini recognised. 'It is heartening to learn that there are others besides myself who agree that one must carry out whichever duty the day demands!'

Locked inside a dazed trance, Tarini watched the unscrupulous old Countess shooing the servants outside to where cars were waiting to transport them to the church, then responded like an automaton to an imperious command to join her outside just as the bridal car glided to a halt at the foot of a flight of stone steps leading up to the castle entrance.

'Get in, child!' the Countess commanded regally, daring her to hesitate.

For the first time since Maria Frick's arrival shock relaxed its grip upon Tarini's vocal chords. 'But, Countess, I ought not to . . . I *can't*. . . .!'

'You *must*!' she mouthed, turning her head aside so that Hans could not witness the glare that would have completely destroyed his air of happy anticipation. Talon-sharp fingers gripped her arm to push her inside the limousine while at the same time the Countess raised her voice loud enough to carry into the hall where Maria Frick was waiting. 'And if anyone should comment upon my absence from the ceremony, please explain that at the last moment I decided I did not feel up to the short journey after all. No one must be allowed to worry about me,' she stressed, including Hans in her look of warning, 'in response to any query, you must state quite truthfully that you left me happy and contented, being entertained by the only person whose company can in any way compensate for the disappointment of missing the ceremony.'

In a state of dazed disbelief, Tarini made no further effort to fight the inevitable. During the short drive to the church she sat transfixed, her mind completely dominated by the old lady's iron determination to allow nothing to interfere with her plan to remove her son out of Maria Frick's magnetic orbit. The pressure of Hans' horny fingers upon her arm barely registered as he helped her out of the car, then ushered her inside the tiny porch of a church set like a shrine upon the mountainside. Nerves began to quiver as the muted tone of an organ drifted from the interior and she stumbled, her limbs suddenly numb, as she approached the threshold.

'Are you all right, *Fräulein*?' Hans' anxious voice sounded very far away. 'How white you are! Shall I ask someone to fetch a glass of water?'

She shook her head. Water could not bring oblivion, could not wash away the guilt of knowing that she could be judged a willing conspirator in a plot to deprive Count Hugo of the woman he loved. For without having to be told, it made sense to assume that Baroness Frick's appearance was indicative of a change of mind, that she had rushed to Schloss Wolke with the sole intention of telling Hugo that she had returned his ring in a fit of pique, that she loved him so much she was prepared to wait until he felt the time was right for them to marry.

Yet not even conscience, it seemed, could interrupt Tarini's slow, tense progress up the aisle. The interior of the church was surprisingly free of decoration, walls of stripped pine ran unbroken from floor to ceiling, pews of the same pale wood, a few clay pots overspilling with colourful flowers which earlier that morning had been opening their chalices to sun pouring over Alpine peaks, ridges, slopes and pastures; wrought iron altar rails, and a large, plain wooden cross set high enough to communicate its message to the entire congregation.

Feeling the condemning eyes of painted images upon her bowed head, she faltered to a halt at the side of the grim-faced Count more soberly dressed than she had ever before seen him, and stood with her cold hand clasped in his, waiting obediently to utter her responses, wondering, as the ruby heart of triumph chilled the curve of her breast, why wearing the supreme accolade had brought none of the happiness, pride and sense of achievement said to have been bestowed upon the fabled 'little weakling'.

'. . . for better, for worse, for richer, for poorer, in sickness and in health . . . I now pronounce you man and wife . . .'

She was jerked out of her trance by the touch of a kindly hand upon her bowed head and looked up in time to see the priest smile before concluding gravely:

'A cold legal agreement cannot hold a marriage together. But love can. As Saint Paul said: "There is nothing love cannot face; there is no limit to its faith, its hope, its endurance". May you both be blessed with real love, affection that grows deeper and deeper, and lasts until the end of time.'

CHAPTER TEN

CONSCIOUS that a sword of Damocles was suspended by a hair above her head, Tarini remained in a state of frozen silence while Count Hugo drove back to Schloss Wolke. The servants had been given the remainder of the day off and with the promise of a celebratory meal at the castle later that evening, had dispersed quite happily to pursue their own particular forms of enjoyment, once they had waved the bridal couple on their way.

As Hugo began nosing the car along a road inclining upwards towards the castle Tarini sought desperately for words to prepare him for the shock of seeing the girl he loved waiting to greet him when he arrived home with his new bride. She ran the tip of her tongue around lips that felt dry, forced a painful swallow, and was just about to blurt out the news when he forestalled her.

'You seem very subdued.' He cast a frown in her direction. 'I'm sorry if you are feeling let down.

With hindsight, I realise that I should have arranged some small celebration—a quiet luncheon, perhaps—because I am aware that women set great store by such things. Also, you deserve to be rewarded for helping me out. I ought to consider myself fortunate,' a laconic smile indicated that he was actually feeling the reverse. 'Husbands, when they are being truthful, often declare that marriage brings shackles which progress from the lightness of a feather to the drag of a ball and chain. By agreeing to enter into a marriage of common interest and mutual profit you have helped me to avoid such a burden. Ours will not be so much a marriage as a business partnership that is bound to prosper because we each have a common aim—to protect an old lady's health—and in the furtherance of that aim we must follow the pattern of all successful business partnerships by agreeing to pool our resources, to trust and be honest with each other, and to share all profits fairly. I shall collect my share of dividends in freedom, in enjoying the liberty to come and go as I please, happy in the knowledge that any crisis that might occur will be competently handled by my partner. Do you realise, Tarini,' he lifted his eyes from the road just long enough to flick her a slightly exasperated glance, 'that you have not yet shown the slightest interest in your own share of the profits? Are you really as unworldly as you appear, or,' his lip curled slightly, 'have you managed to conclude without any help from me that as well as achieving the status of a wife and ensuring lifelong security, that as Countess von Triesen you stand to reap the benefits of a quite considerable family fortune?'

'Wealth doesn't interest me,' she told him simply, the evenness of her tone contradicted by the rapid rise and fall of the jewel pendant splashed like a drop of heart's blood against a milk-white curve of breast.

'Of course it doesn't.' His mockery thrust sharp as a whetted blade. 'How remiss of me to need reminding that you are one of a sex devoted to the easing of men's misery! Today especially, having lived through the experience of watching you falter down the aisle encompassed by an aura of innocence, of hearing you chant your responses in the manner of a first-time sinner seeking absolution, I should not be finding it so difficult to believe that you would have acted as generously had I been a peasant whose wife would be able to look forward to no more than a life of drudgery and a home in the mountains offering none of the comfort and refinement you have so quickly learned to appreciate during your stay in Schloss Wolke.'

Mindful of retribution looming close as witch-hat turrets piercing the clouds above the castle, she gasped a last, desperate plea.

'It was you who saw marriage as a release from bondage, Count Hugo—you who laid down the conditions!'

His startled silence lasted until he drew the car to a halt at the foot of the castle steps. Impulsively, Tarini snatched at the door handle, anxious to make her escape, then drew back feeling cornered, daunted by the prospect of what she might be called upon to face once she stepped across the threshold.

'I'm sorry, Tarini,' his sigh echoed the heaviness of her own heart, 'you are quite right to remind me that mistakes, even those that arise when emotion is allowed to overrule reason, cannot be rectified by regret. We have passed the halfway mark, that last split second when an error can be recognised and perhaps cancelled. The blame is entirely mine—I proposed in haste, therefore the least I can do is try to ensure that your leisure time is not entirely taken up with repentance.'

Any sort of reply was beyond her. Shaking with nerves, she preceded him up the steps, then hesitated, her obvious reluctance to enter the castle causing him to frown.

Suddenly he swooped, plucking her light as thistledown into his arms. 'Just as the "little weakling" won the right to wear her emblem of triumph,' he murmured tightly, eyeing the ruby pulsating frantically over her heart, 'you, too, have won the right to the sort of reward expected by every romantic young bride whose illusions would be shattered were her bridegroom to omit carrying her across the threshold!'

Oblivious to the fact that her tension was caused by terror, he carried her inside the hall into which, any second, she expected a furious Baroness Frick to erupt babbling recriminations, accusing herself and the Countess of collusion, of deliberately keeping her in ignorance of the impending wedding ceremony.

But when a door was flung open just as Hugo was lowering her to her feet, she saw Maria Frick tripping lightly towards them, warmly smiling.

'At last, Hugo darling! I've been waiting simply ages . . .!'

At the sound of her voice his head jerked erect and at that precise moment the Baroness halted in her tracks, her smile fading, wide eyes questioning his role in the tableau of a bridegroom carrying his bride into her new home.

The hiss of his indrawn breath rasped across Tarini's tortured nerves, as did the ragged edge to his voice; his expression of inarticulate hunger.

'Maria! What the devil are you doing here . . .?'

A moan froze in Tarini's throat when, as his mother stepped smiling into the arena, she began vaguely to perceive a depth of cruelty that was enabling the old Countess to savour a scene deliberately set in order to gain the maximum satisfaction from her enemy's downfall.

'Ah, Tarini!' she flung welcoming arms wide. 'Come here, my dear, I can't wait to kiss the bride.'

When no one moved, no one seemed capable of so much as expelling a breath, she swung round, wicked eyes sparkling, to taunt the stunned Austrian beauty.

'Surely, dear Baroness,' mocking eyebrows rose, 'I did not omit to mention that when my son arrived home he would be accompanied by his wife, the brand-new Countess von Triesen?'

Eight hours later the horror of that moment had still not faded. As Tarini sat shivering in the room she had occupied since leaving her hotel two weeks previously, pictures were flashing continuously in her mind's eye—a beautiful face that looked stricken, blue eyes wide with shock, dazed disbelief. An older, deeply-wrinkled face made ugly by a vengeful smile of triumph. And worst of all, the blank, unreadable expression of a man too proud to reveal the true extent of damage inflicted by a blow that had knocked him speechless, that had scored deep lines of anger either side of his tightly compressed mouth, that had darkened green eyes to the depths of dangerous, swirling torrents.

She had felt plunged into a pool of melted ice when his glittering green glare had swung her way and had gasped, her breath cut off by the shock of cold dislike projected into his brief, damning question:

'You knew about Maria's arrival before you left for the church?'

'Not only did she know, she must have guessed that the reason behind my visit was to try to effect a reconciliation!' Maria Frick had almost screamed, looking ready to rake pointed fingernails down Tarini's guilty face. 'Why else,' she had whirled upon Hugo to toss the stormy question, 'would she have helped your mother to deliberately mislead me, to foster the illusion that the wedding about to take place was that of a servant! Had the bride been anyone other than this pale-faced, quivering mouse who has somehow managed to catch you on the rebound, Hugo, they would not have found me half so easy to deceive! We have been duped, my darling,' suddenly her hard, angry stare had been softened by a rush of vexed tears, 'our happiness ruined by two conniving females prepared to sink to any depths in order to keep us apart!'

Agitated to the point of feeling ill, Tarini jumped to her feet and began pacing the tiny, circular tower bedroom which many centuries previously had been used to house prisoners who had aroused the wrath of the reigning Count von Triesen. In spite of the warmth of her sensible dressing-gown she shivered and tightened the belt around her waist as for the very first time the spiral stone staircase leading up to her room; the roughcast walls, the stone floor with a hardness barely disguised by luxurious carpets; the narrow stained-glass window; the faint inscriptions scratched by prisoners into panelling black with age, adopted a menacing significance. Scornful of its modern accoutrements, the castle in the clouds had managed to retain a musty smell of antiquity in keeping with walls and passageways hung with relics of a barbaric age when wood and chain fetters had been used to hobble sentenced women; when men's flesh had been branded with white-hot iron, their shoulders bruised with the weight of wooden yokes, a time during which offenders had been executed without trial, despatched from the face of the earth with one blow from the mighty sword of Triesen!

She had become so wound up with worry, so tense and edgy, that when a sound broke the silence she twirled to face the door, fighting back a frightened scream. While she had been pacing, daylight had gradually dimmed so that she was barely able to discern the latch lifting slowly before the heavy wooden door began swinging inward.

'Who's there . . .?' she quavered, aware that the servants always knocked then awaited permission to enter. 'What do you want?'

'Merely a husband come in search of his wife,' a voice responded, dangerously dry, soft as the footsteps that began advancing towards the centre of the room. 'Shortly, we will be expected to make an appearance before the servants, but, knowing the unwordly innocence of my shy young bride, I thought it wise to begin with a short private celebration of our own.'

She heard the snap of a switch before light flooded from a lamp that threw sparks from diamond-studded cuffs, its steady beam making an elegant form out of the silver tray holding two crystal glasses and a dark green bottle, foiled with gold around its neck, which he slid on to a table.

'C . . . Count Hugo!' she stammered, unable to meet a condemning stare projecting a message that she was living dangerously, that she was in the presence of a man intent as a wounded eagle upon revenging his pain and humiliation upon the nearest vulnerable throat.

'Now that our business contract has been rendered null and void, don't you think it's time you began calling me Hugo—or even Hugo darling, if you prefer?'

'I . . . I'm not sure what you are implying.' She stared, subconsciously seeking protection from threat by clutching the collar of her dressing gown tighter around her throat.

'Come now, Tarini,' he mocked, paying lazy attention to the task of peeling protective foil from the slender-necked bottle, 'surely you aren't going to deny that even while you were appending your signature to our marriage contract you had already broken one of the main clauses of our agreement? *To trust and be honest with each other*,' he stressed silkily, then betrayed hidden ferocity by gouging hard thumbs into the cork so that it exploded from its resting place with a report that had the effect upon Tarini's nerves of a loud, sharp pistol shot.

Expertly, he tipped frothing, golden liquid into each of the glasses, then handed her one. 'Take it!' he snapped, sensing the refusal hovering on her lips. 'A marriage must always be celebrated with champagne; it is a wine that provides a sense of occasion; a drink that can either bring people together or tear them apart.'

Too terrified to refuse, she carried the glass to her lips in shaking fingers and gasped at the sting of bubbles bursting beneath her nose. Resisting an impulse to sneeze, she gulped down a mouthful, then almost choked when deliberately he tilted up her glass, tipping a stream of iced, raw gold down her unsuspecting throat. The result of his cruel action was a paroxysm of coughing that left her with eyes streaming, her limbs shaking with reaction.

'Fiend . . .!' she finally managed to croak, then backed hastily into a corner when he began advancing with the champagne bottle in his extended hand. 'Please, no more,' she pleaded, 'you know it makes me ill!'

Steadying her nerveless fingers around the glass,

he filled it once more to the brim, then ordered grimly: 'Drink up—this is the surest way I know of loosening your tongue!'

Hating him with her eyes, she had no choice but to submit to his will and drain the glass dry.

'Now,' he pushed her into a chair and leant close to glower into her dazed eyes, 'tell me the truth! Exactly why did you condone my mother's wickedness by carrying on with the wedding even though Maria's arrival must have given sufficient indication that she had had a change of heart?'

'The Countess was so insistent,' she gasped, groping for control over befuddled senses. The wine was already coursing madness through her veins, daring her to giggle, soaring her spirits so that she felt wafted from her chair, afloat inside a great golden bubble, drowning her natural reserve until she was tempted to blurt out that she had married him because she was in love with him, but mainly because five minutes in Baroness Frick's company had been sufficient to convert her to his mother's point of view that true beauty should be a glow from within, a reflection of inner goodness, not merely a visual feast such as that offered by the vain peacock or the aloof, unbending lily.

'The truth, as I see it, pious little fraud,' the indictment speared through her euphoric daze, 'is that you could not bear to see a heaven-sent chance of security slipping out of your grasp! Couldn't you have trusted me to ensure that honesty would have been well rewarded? He shook her until she felt bruised. 'Did you have to employ deceit, build castles in the air that were fated to tumble to the ground?'

He released her as if stung and strode across to the bed where her wedding gown lay gossamer-soft, folded neatly as the wings of an exhausted butterfly.

'Time once again to don your mantle of innocence!' She smothered a cry of distress when the dress he flung towards her billowed in the air, then sank soft as a sigh into her lap. 'You plotted your way into the role of Countess, so you shall play out your part to the bitter end. Get dressed,' he commanded coldly, 'you must be taught the lessons of duty. The foremost art required of those in positions of authority is the power to keep one's countenance, to appear composed even when faced with calamity. You have taken what you wanted—*now you must pay*!'

The potency of champagne is released in easy stages, upon the tongue, the roof of the mouth, the throat, then finally the senses. By the time Tarini was ready to carry out her first task as Countess von Triesen she was feeling grateful for the false glow of wellbeing that made it possible to animate her stiff limbs, to chat, to smile, even to sparkle, as she circulated among happy servants who had gathered to extend their good wishes and to toast the health of their employer and his charming, endearingly shy young bride.

A festive atmosphere filled the room that had been chosen for the reception. Flowers were spilling from vases set in every niche and upon every window ledge; coloured ribbons were strewn across picture frames, bunched around ornaments, and hung from the ceiling to form a colourful, shimmering backcloth for a small band of musicians whose instruments had been momentarily discarded while their owners joined in what seemed to be a particularly hilarious party game. Tables were groaning beneath a weight of sausages and hams; salted beef, potato cakes, fritters, tarts, and rich gâteaux filled with hazelnuts, walnuts, cream and honey, some decorated with tiny marzipan carrots, others flavoured with kirsch distilled from cherries grown in local orchards.

Once everyone had taken the opportunity to extend their good wishes to the bridal pair, Hans gravitated to Tarini's side, frowning slightly at the lost, helpless look he saw when he discovered her abandoned by her bridegroom.

'So, already you have become a ski-widow, Countess!' He nodded towards Hugo standing a few feet away engrossed in conversation with a man whose tough, leathered look indicated that his natural habitat was out-of-doors. 'A foretaste of what to expect once the winter season is upon us,' Hans smiled a warning. 'When he was just an infant I made your husband his first pair of skis and took him for a lesson on the nursery slopes. Since then, until he met you, of course,' he amended jocularly, 'skiing has been his main obsession, his one abiding passion.'

With the exception of Maria Frick! Tarini thought sadly.

Disturbed by the pensive cloud that had descended upon her delicate features, Hans cupped her elbow within his horny palm and began urging her towards a group of guests gathered in a circle around some source of great hilarity.

'Come, you must sample the fondue—an inspired dish made up of Swiss cheese, Swiss wine, and Swiss kirsch that forms both a meal and a party game.'

Without demur she allowed him to lead her into the centre of the group sitting around a large earthenware fondue dish in which a creamy cheese mixture was slowly bubbling, kept hot by a spirit heater placed directly under the bowl. Each guest had a long-handled fork and a plate. Baskets of fresh bread cubes were being passed around, and amid much giggling and goodnatured chaffing bread cubes were being speared on to forks dipped into the cheese, then transferred quickly into gaping mouths before the melted cheese could begin to drip.

'Anyone who loses his bread in the dip must pay a forfeit,' Hans chuckled. 'Traditionally, a man will pay with a round of drinks, but a woman is expected to discharge her debt with a kiss, especially if she is attractive!'

A long-handled fork with a cube of bread attached was pushed into Tarini's hand, then, encouraged by much laughter and shouted instructions, she dipped it into the bubbling cheese until the bread was well covered before slowly and carefully withdrawing the fork in an attempt to retrieve the tasty morsel. Flushed and excited by the success of her efforts, she was just about to negotiate the fork over the rim of the dish when the cube of bread slipped off the prongs and fell with a plop into the cheese mixture.

'A kiss, a kiss—the bride must pay a forfeit!'

Resigned to settling her debt, she swung round laughing in search of a recipient, then jolted with shock when she saw that the crowd of guests had mischievously parted so that the nearest male available was her approaching husband.

'A kiss, a kiss, the bride must pay a forfeit!' the laughing crowd chanted, urging her forward.

There was no way of escape, no alternative but to slip inside the circle of Hugo's reluctantly extended arms, then stand on tiptoe to bestow an embarrassed peck. But within full view of their expectant audience, Hugo had no choice but to play up to the role of eager bridegroom. As her shy lips brushed lightly as a moth across his unsmiling mouth she glimpsed a savage flash of green behind devil-dark lashes, felt a talon-tight grip upon her waist, before his mouth descended to crush the protest from lips retaining the bitter-sweetness of wine he had vowed would either draw them together or tear them apart.

Immediately his lips touched hers her heart plummeted into an abyss, then with a breathtaking whoosh soared upwards, high as white-covered peaks made blinding by sunshine, poised as a ski-jumper hovering for a lifetime between earth and sky before swooping downwards, hurling into the blue with violent impetus.

When he lifted his head she landed with a bump, feeling limp, shaken to the core by the shocking experience. As if conscious of her helplessness, her inability to speak, to move, or even to catch her breath, he responded by scooping her into his arms and retreating towards the door with his fragile burden.

'My wife is exhausted,' he called across his shoulder to their delighted guests. 'I hope you will excuse us if we retire early!'

Tarini returned to blushing normality only after he had carried her up the flight of marble stairs, along a passageway, then slowed to a halt outside an unfamiliar door.

'Please put me down!' She squirmed with panic aroused by a glimpse of a determined, square-cut jaw, shocked by the reminder of a remark she had allowed to pass without comment because at the time its threat had barely registered: *'You have taken what you wanted—now you must pay!'*

Ignoring her protest, Hugo carried her inside a bedroom whose interior appeared subdued as a temple, dappled with mosaic shadows being cast by a full moon beaming through a large stained glass window. His intention became clear when he lowered her on to a massive double bed, slid the shoes from her feet, then began calmly and unemotionally to undo the row of tiny mother-of-pearl buttons fastening the bodice of her dress.

'We . . . we agreed to a business arrangement,' she stormed, eyes dark as shadow-hugging gentians.

'Which you conveniently ignored the moment you appeared to be in danger of losing a husband,' he reminded her through lips thinned into a straight line of cruelty. 'You plotted to become a wife, and a wife is exactly what I intend you shall become—but if your innocence shies from the act of consummation, little hypocrite, then try regarding me as a father confessor come to help absolve you of the sin of matrimonial trickery by imposing a fitting penance!'

CHAPTER ELEVEN

RELUCTANTLY, in the manner of a prisoner grown fond of her cell, Tarini gathered up the last of her belongings to transfer them from the tower room into the bedroom she had begun to hate, the room in which every night for the past week Hugo had joined her with the object of claiming his marital rights, to impose the diabolical punishment he had deemed a fitting sentence for her crime.

'I am no celibate!' She flinched even now from the reminder of his mocking words. 'To a hungry man, bread and cheese can be as satisfying as a banquet.'

With cheeks flamed by humiliation, she stumbled blindly out of the tower room clasping an armful of clothing, and almost dropped them in fright when Hugo's voice speared sharp and cutting immediately she stepped inside the room that might have appealed as a sanctuary were it not for the devil in residence.

'Can't you break the habit of servitude? How often must I remind you that it upsets the servants to see the Gräfin von Triesen taking over their duties?'

'I'm sorry,' she mumbled, backing nervously away from his prowling masculinity. 'It's force of habit, I'm afraid—I can't get used to the idea of asking a servant to do a job I'm perfectly capable of doing myself. I feel so useless,' she frowned. 'Even your mother no longer seems inclined to make use of my services.'

'Because she has been warned that they are no longer available,' he retorted, stalking the space she had carefully kept between them.

'But . . . but she needs me,' Tarini gasped, unable to remove her eyes from a face sending cold thrills of fear down her spine. 'Surely that was the whole purpose of the exercise?'

'Exactly as I thought!' His eagle profile sharpened. 'Exactly as I was meant to think. But, miraculously, my mother, whose history of heart attacks can be traced back to the moment she became aware of my attachment to Maria, has recovered sufficiently to declare herself well enough to spend a short holiday with a friend in Vaduz. Either she has wisely decided to adopt a low profile, to remove her uneasy conscience from the vicinity of the son she has helped to dupe, or she is being diplomatic,' he drawled with a suavity that caused Tarini's heart to jolt, 'even an unscrupulous, interfering, over-possessive mother must realise that her presence is superfluous on a honeymoon.'

'Honeymoon . . .?' She almost choked on the word. 'Is that what you call our . . . our sexual coupling?'

She wanted to shrivel up and die when he tossed

back his head and laughed aloud, glorying in the success of the punishment he had inflicted—a punishment that had left no visible scars, unless one counted the haunted look in eyes bruised as velvet gentian petals after a shower of hail, or a slender-stemmed body crushed by the weight of an uncaring foot.

'Even little weaklings can spring surprises,' he taunted, sounding driven to cruelty by her refusal to condemn, his iced-green stare willing her gentle mouth to quiver, her eyes to flood with tears, so that he might extract satisfaction from the loss of her uncanny composure. 'Do you know, Tarini, that you purr like a kitten when you are stroked? That your claws turn to velvet and your tense, arched resistance crumples at exactly the right moment into sensuous, writhing capitulation?'

'Stop it!' With a cry that was more of a whimper she tried to snap the chain of bondage by spinning away from her tormentor and burying burning cheeks in hands quivering beneath a weight of shame and humiliation.

'What's wrong, Tarini?' he snarled softly. 'Are you regretting depriving your rival of her rightful crown, hoping, perhaps, that your judge might be merciful enough to allow the remainder of your punishment to be doled out with a whip?'

'You call that a choice?' He could barely make out the whispered, broken words. 'Could any thong cut deeper than your steel-tipped tongue?'

'What right has a pretender to expect mercy?' Though she would not look into his face, the harshness of his voice supplied ample evidence of resentment seething molten-hot beneath an icy exterior. 'Can any man be condemned for withholding loyalty from a prevaricating wife who charted a zig-zag course to the altar and mouthed crooked responses before a man of God?'

Stung out of her misery by the unjust accusation, she turned slowly to challenge the man who had changed innocence into guilt, virtue into vice, the husband who, with wanton expertise, had taught a timid dove the way to satisfy the appetite of a hungry eagle.

'Baroness Frick has sworn that she will never give you up, Hugo, that she intends to stay here in Liechtenstein so as to be near at hand when you grow tired of walking the straight, narrow road of matrimony. So why not put all three of us out of our misery by arranging a quick divorce?' she suggested as bravely as she was able, considering the very thought of losing him was tearing the heart out of her body.

'You can discard that idea immediately!' His swift, savage rejection aroused confused emotions of pain, relief and comfort. 'Divorce is an admission of failure. No member of my family has ever been known to lay down his arms nor to retreat from battle. Wedlock or deadlock—whichever word you choose to describe our marriage, the fact remains that it is a life sentence, with no remission for either partner in the crime!'

The tears he had deliberately provoked spurted into her eyes as, keeping her head bowed, she nervously twisted the broad gold band lying heavy as a fetter around her finger, grieving over the amount of misery contained inside the wedding ring embossed with symbols of myrtle sprigs to encourage fertility, and edelweiss, the delicate flower conditioned to a harsh environment, that managed to bloom even under a cover of snow and with the warmth engendered by its frail body succeeded in melting the ice of winter's cold embrace.

Perhaps every devil is not entirely without conscience, or again, it might have been that even Hugo's ice-encrusted heart was moved by the sight of blue-velvet eyes moistened with misery, of a brave mouth distorted by a painful quiver, of a stem-slim body drooping as if buffeted by stormy emotions. On his way towards the door he paused, then slowly retraced his steps until he was once more towering, oppressive as the Eiger, over her downbent head.

'I'm going windsurfing, would you like to come?'

His softly voiced question affected her like a snarl. Her head jerked upright, searching for the glint of cruelty, for the sardonic twist of his lips she had learned to expect, and found them absent. Suspicious of sheathed claws, of a growl reduced to a throaty purr, she backed out of reach of the unpredictable Alpine prowler.

'I would only be in your way,' she swallowed painfully.

'In which case, I'd probably gobble you up in one bite, which is what you seem to be expecting at this very moment,' he returned drily. 'Am I such an ogre, Tarini, that you cannot contemplate sharing a few hours of civilised enjoyment in my company?'

For a second she was tempted to remind him that his conduct, since their wedding day, had been far from civilised, more reminiscent of the barbaric attitude adopted by his ancestors in the Middle Ages, but just in time she managed to swallow the bitter accusation when hope sprang eternal as the Alpine rose from its rocky bed.

'Then if you're sure you won't find me too indigestible,' she dimpled, 'I'd love to come.'

It was sheer bliss knowing that for once her presence was not resented as Hugo drove down the spiralling mountain road with the scent of pine and the perfume of meadow flowers drifting through the open windows, and the tinkle of cowbells making music in the warm, still air. The magnificence of the Alps soared all around them, then gradually receded towards the horizon when they reached the floor of the valley and began travelling along the cobbled streets of unspoiled villages lined with cuckoo-clock houses aglow with painted murals, gardens crammed with flowers, balconies draped with duvets whipped off beds to air. In many of the gardens old men were busy replenishing depleted stocks of kindling, cutting each piece of firewood to a precise thickness and length, then stacking them so that the cut ends formed an artistic mosaic that added to the attraction of each picturesque chalet.

'Alpine races are so methodical in everything they do,' she commented without thinking, reminded of the insistence upon split-second punctuality that had contributed to the trauma of her missed flight. 'I'm prepared to believe that here babies are born to a regulation weight and length and that they arrive with a stop-watch clutched in a tiny fist.'

After a startled pause Hugo surprised her by laughing aloud. 'We are not saints, but we do keep our appointments and our promises,' he glinted wickedly. 'Unlike you English who believe that delay is preferable to error, we live each day as if the sun might not rise tomorrow.'

'What a sobering thought!' Instinctively, she shuddered from the ideal of being deprived one last sight of chiffon scarves of mist slowly dispersing around dew-soaked peaks; of awakening to the thrill of a sleep-softened profile lying bronzed as the head of a coin against a snow-white pillow. 'If you were to be somehow convinced that this day was to be the last,' she pondered thoughtfully, 'how would you want to spend it?'

Her fingers curled into tight fists of anxiety as she waited, already regretting the question that must have flooded his mind with thoughts of the girl he loved, the one who had claimed the primary place in his affections. Chancing a sideways glance, she deduced from his look of concentration that he was treating her question with great seriousness. She was almost on the point of blurting that it did not matter, that it was pointless searching for a reply tactful enough to avoid hurting her feelings, when he shocked her by confessing:

'I would probably spend it trying to make my peace with you, little weakling. I'm not a particularly superstitious person, nor am I a devoutly religious one, therefore I'm forced to conclude that cowardice is the motive behind my aversion to stepping into the great unknown burdened by an uneasy conscience. *Have* I wronged you, Tarini?' His frown betrayed indecision. 'Could *you* anticipate eternity without suffering remorse?'

'I'm no more a paragon than you are a coward,' she blushed, feeling ridiculously lighthearted without having the faintest inkling why. There had been no single word, no shift of attitude to encourage such optimism, yet a lightening of the atmosphere, something about the quirk playing around his mouth, about eyes reminding her of fireflies dancing over the surface of a placid green lake, kindled warmth within the cold, dark void where her heart was buried and brought to her wide, trusting eyes the glow of gratitude shown by a child who has been slapped and then quickly forgiven.

They ate a snack lunch of salami, mountain ham, cheese, bread and fresh fruit in a restaurant overlooking a lake, then drove towards an adjacent town no larger than a village, made up mainly of guesthouses and shops stacked with goods to attract the custom of summer visitors.

'You'll need a wet-suit.' Minutes after leaving the car Hugo paused in front of a sports shop window. 'One of good quality that is close-fitting yet soft and flexible. I take it you *can* swim?'

'Yes,' Tarini nodded, 'although I haven't had much opportunity since leaving school.'

'All that is needed to become reasonably proficient at windsurfing is an ability to stand up and maintain one's balance. Learners, however, spend most of their time falling into the water, clambering back on to their boards, and starting again, but if you possess sufficient stubbornness and resistance to soakings, skill will follow, together with the thrill and exhilaration of skimming across the lake, pitting your wits against variable winds.'

As well as a wet-suit—chosen, at Hugo's insistence, because it was the exact shade of blue as her eyes—they purchased a pair of warm, non-slip shoes that could be easily kicked off and added as an afterthought a harness to be used as a buoyancy aid while she learned to cope with the pull of the sail.

'I suppose,' she dared to tease as she settled back into the car to be driven to a private boathouse situated on the far, more secluded, shore of the lake, 'that you windsurf as expertly as you ski?'

'I do enjoy the challenge of guiding a masted surfboard round slalom-type courses, and striving to achieve better and faster speeds, but I cannot yet claim to have reached Olympic standards,' he responded as smoothly as he slipped the car into gear. 'You might say that I have become passionately addicted to the sport, that I am drawn, as always,' he concluded in a murmur, 'towards any mysterious unknown that calls for cautious exploration, for risky experiments that often result in failure but hold out the hope of eventual mastery.'

Mastery! The same sort of mastery he had employed to elevate her own sparrow-brown modesty to a flaming-flamingo flaunt! She turned her head aside, hoping he would overlook her painful blush. Defeat was an anathema to the Count von Triesen, who would be satisfied with nothing less than entire possession, complete dominance, especially over any woman who bore his name. She suffered a shiver contradictory as ice-capped peaks shimmering beneath hot blue sky. He had stripped her body of vanity, exposed her emotions to ridicule; had revenged his humiliation by treating her like a plaything, an inanimate object that could be used, broken, and discarded at a whim. Yet because of her aptitude for mental retreat, her ability to find refuge from physical pain in the ivory towers of her mind, she had cheated him out of the satisfaction of breaking her pride. Did he resent her secret hoard of privacy? Was revenge so rampant that he would not rest content until he had forced her to swallow the last bitter dregs of reality?

Within the following hours everything combined to make her feel ashamed of such an unworthy suspicion. It was as if the wet-suits they had donned became a uniform for sheer enjoyment, so nearly identical she felt Hugo had been levelled from aristocratic heights to the plane of ordinary mortals like herself who, without any sort of position to maintain, could laugh hilariously, tease with complete spontaneity, play with outrageous abandonment. He seemed to have decided that their checkmate contest should be abandoned, that the king and the pawn should be slotted into a box that rendered them equal.

'Steady. . . .!' His clutch upon her waist barely registered upon her senses as she concentrated upon keeping her balance on the bobbing surfboard and upon following his concise instructions: 'Always remember to start with your back to the wind—one foot forward of the mast and the other on the daggerboard slot. Now, bend your knees slightly and begin hauling up the line, using the knots as handholds!'

Nervously at first, then with growing confidence she did as he had directed until the sail resting flat upon the surface of the lake began swinging clear of the water.

'Good girl!' His approval went to her head like champagne.

'Oh, I'm moving!' she gasped. *'Hugo . . .!'* Exhilarated by the panicky sensation caused by the board beneath her feet responding to the impetus of a windblown sail, she screamed for help. 'Hold me, hold me, I know I'm going to fall!'

'Keep your body upright—don't bend forward!' he yelled across the gap rapidly widening between herself and the shore. But even as he yelled Tarini felt her knees buckling beneath her. Losing all sense of co-ordination, she let slip the rope controlling the angle of inclination of the mast, so that the sail sighed down upon the surface of the lake, leaving her with arms flailing, body rocking for one frantic second before she lost her balance completely and plunged into the water.

She had imagined she had travelled quite a distance from shore, yet within a matter of seconds she swam into shallows. Breathless, bedraggled, she hauled herself ashore, then paused, still knee-deep in water, to glare indignantly at Hugo who was bent double by a paroxysm of laughter.

'Only the malevolent can find amusement in the misfortune of others!' she spluttered furiously. Overlooking the drag of the water, the suck of shingle, she made to spurt angrily towards him, then was checked, as if by hands holding fast to her ankles, while the rest of her body was carried on by impetus throwing her with a smack, face-first in the shallows.

'Tarini, are you hurt?' In spite of having difficulty controlling his mirth, Hugo looked anxious as he dragged her out of the shingle and tilted her chin to examine her face for bruises. Once he had assured himself that her only facial blemish was a row of angry freckles his grin reappeared, yet his look was no longer teasing, more concerned—even serious.

'No doubt about it, you are a plucky little imp,' he murmured, massaging his thumbs across the curve of her shoulders in a manner that was almost caressing. 'Would you be prepared to begin again from the beginning, Tarini? Sometimes a limp can be forgotten, even disappear completely, if one keeps on walking.'

As they stared at each other in silence, exchanging intense, startled looks of exploration, she sensed instinctively that the question was in no way connected with windsurfing, that he was teetering on the brink of some discovery so delicate, so important to them both, that one unwary word, one thoughtless action, might snap the first delicate thread inserted into a tapestry consisting, as yet, of no more than the faint outline of a story of true love and nuptial bliss, as well as the promise of delight too dazzling to contemplate should the tapestry ever be completed.

'Well, Tarini?' The fresh, masculine, faintly-rubbery smell of his wet-suit caught in her throat when he pulled her towards him. 'Which lesson would you like to learn next—shall we concentrate upon altering course, or would you prefer to bear away?'

His arms tightened slowly, drawing her nearer. His head lowered, blotting out mountains and sky as his mouth hovered over hers, awaiting some signal—a modest sweep of lashes across flushed cheeks, a hushed sigh of surrender, the slightest movement of invitation from her trembling body—that would give him permission to drive out the devil of frustration with kisses.

'*Hallooo!* Hugo, *mein liebchen*, I'm over here!'

As the call shattered their privacy Hugo stiffened, then slowly turned to watch a motor launch containing half a dozen people heading towards the shore.

'Maria!' He expelled her name like a curse on an angry breath. 'How the devil did she know we were here!'

Uninvited or not, their visitors had obviously come prepared for a prolonged stay. Immediately the boat berthed inside the boathouse Maria and her two female companions made a beeline for Hugo, while their escorts followed in their wake carrying hampers and a cool box containing bottles of champagne.

'Surprise, surprise!' Maria ran smiling to throw her arms around Hugo, turning her back upon Tarini so that she was firmly relegated to the position of a ringsider allowed to watch but not to participate in the main event. 'As we were scouring the shore for a likely spot to picnic we just happened to catch sight of you, *liebling*. So naturally, as soon as we realised that you were in difficulties, we came immediately to your rescue!'

Hugo had no option but to be polite, to welcome their visitors warmly, Tarini assured herself time and time again during the duration of an outing that had changed as suddenly as alpine weather from sparkling blue to dull, depressing grey.

As she lay sunbathing on the shore, looking and feeling like a discarded plaything, jealousy gnawed her inside as, skulking behind dark glasses, she watched Maria and her friends displaying elegant expertise on their windsurfing boards, guiding, tacking, curving towards and away from the wind without so much as a splash of spray to dampen their enthusiasm.

Maria paused once in passing to rake a contemptuous look over the slender, sparrow-boned girl who had dared to snatch the man she had been determined to marry. Her eyes were fastened upon Hugo, who was skimming across the lake with athletic ease when she jeered softly down at Tarini:

'A dozen times I almost lost him to rivals far more seductive than yourself. When the novelty of your wide-eyed innocence wears off, how can you hope to hold him, a philandering rake, a mountain Adonis who, whether speeding across the surface of a lake or skiing down the side of a mountain, betrays an animal thirst for freedom?'

When she moved away with a complacent smile

Tarini felt shrouded by a cloud of doubt and depression, convinced that Maria's assumption was correct and that her own previous suspicion that Hugo's unusual attitude had been inspired by some hidden motive was justified.

Which was why, when he tired of his pastime and began making his way towards her, she tensed, and inched warily away when he eased his lithe body alongside her.

'Maria has invited us to join her party for dinner at her hotel this evening,' he informed her lazily. 'Would you like to go?'

'No, I would not!' She jumped up trembling and for the life of her could not prevent herself from raking feline claws through the flimsy fabric of deceit she had foolishly mistaken for a tapestry designed to portray the sowing, nurturing, and final glorious blossoming of love. 'And please don't insult my intelligence by suggesting that Baroness Frick will be upset by my absence when we are both aware of how greedily she covets your exclusive company, how she adores to bask in the charm you radiate, a charm which in my opinion—an opinion formed during the course of bitter experience—deserves to be rated no higher than the ruthless virility of a farmyard rooster!'

Appalled by her own temerity, she watched his whip-lean body tense, watched him jump to his feet showing the leashed resentment of a proud aristocrat whose habits had just been unfavourably compared with those of a farmyard rooster.

Not even Maria dared to question aloud the motive behind his tight-lipped departure, but

Tarini glimpsed triumph in her eyes as she was bundled into the car, read rejoicing in the complacent manner in which she waved them goodbye.

The seething silence he maintained during their drive back to the castle was a test of endurance that almost broke her spirit. Immediately he drew the car to a halt at the foot of the castle steps she flung open the door and sped without a backward glance up to her bedroom where she quickly stripped off her clothes and stepped under the shower, hoping that sharp, cool needles of water might help to rid her of guilt, might wash away the tarnish of jealousy and envy she was suffering for the very first time in her life.

Hugo appeared to be following suit, for as she sat by a window towelling her hair dry she heard sounds of movement coming from inside his bathroom—the crash of a glazed shower door being thrust aside, thumps from an ill-used cabinet, then finally a curse so audible it made her toes curl.

Her heart leapt with fear, then began beating an erratic tattoo beneath the light silk of her dressing-gown when the connecting door was flung open and he strode over the threshold darkly glowering, his hair tousled, damp patches darkening the crimson towelling of his bathrobe.

'I forgot to mention that in spite of your burst of ill humour, I've assured Maria that we will be delighted to accept her invitation to dine at her hotel this evening,' he spat, a nerve kicking madly in his cheek. 'Consider it your first official engagement,' with hands thrust deep into his pockets he strolled to tower over her crouched, dejected figure, 'that way, you might manage to summon a little of the dignified composure which, up to the present, has been noticeably absent in the new Countess von Triesen!'

Knowing herself to be incapable of facing such an ordeal, yet too terrified to show open defiance, she attempted to placate the tiger growling inside him.

'I'm sorry I spoiled a wonderful day, Hugo.' She cleared her throat in a nervous gulp and concentrated upon pleating the pale pink frill edging the shawl collar of her dressing-gown, 'what I said to you was unforgivable.'

'Yes, wasn't it!' He swooped to pluck her out of her chair and set her down roughly in front of him. With his tight grasp bruising her trembling shoulders he glared: 'I could more easily have suspected a sweet-faced chamois-doe of hidden fangs than have believed you capable of such venom. What went wrong, Tarini—did the effort of being pleasant to the husband you hate suddenly become to much of a strain?'

'I don't hate you, Hugo!' Her softly-gasped denial eased a little of the hardness from his chipped features, relaxed the tightness of his grasp as he drew her slight, shivering figure close enough to feel the heat emanating from his sinewed body.

'You keep your emotions so well hidden, I've never been able to fathom exactly how you do feel about me, Tarini.' Slowly, expertly, he ran the tips of his fingers along the length of her sensitive spine. 'There are only two emotions worth considering,' his silky skein of words were weaving her senses into a hypnotised tangle. 'If it is not hatred you feel for me, can it be love?'

It would have been so easy to have allowed her weary head to droop against the expanse of chest left exposed by powerful muscles flexing beneath the towelled robe, so comforting to have felt once again the stroke of coffee-coloured skin against her cheek, to have surrendered, as she always had done, to the pull of animal magnetism that enabled her to forget her inadequacies and respond to his demands with the confidence of a vital, caring, passionate, tender, shy yet eager bride. But already he was too confident of his mastery; to have admitted her love would have meant committing her soul into the hands of a passionate tyrant. So she fought with a strength culled from the certainty that he saw her as no more than a slave whose spirit he had pledged himself to break and forced a lie past quivering lips.

'I . . . I quite like you, Hugo.'

'Like!' Suddenly he released her and stepped back a pace to hiss: 'Like is not an emotion, more a Limbo that cowards escape to when their placid existence seems threatened. I'd much prefer to be hated,' he scowled, brooding, black-browed and ruthlessly satanic, 'even though, in order to earn that hatred, I'd have to endure sharing a bed with an angel of innocence who, because she has vowed to be a dutiful wife, submits to being defiled by passion's pitch!'

His accusation was so deliberately hurtful, so patently unfair, Tarini choked out the wounded reminder: 'I apologise for my inadequacies, but should you really be surprised by the discovery that a novice cannot achieve the distinction of a performer as practised as, say, Baroness Frick? It was very wrong of me to allow your mother's determined will to influence me into a marriage I knew to be wrong. If only I'd had courage equal to my convictions——' she sighed so quietly his dark head lowered to catch words husked through a tightly constricted throat, 'as it is, there is nothing left to add except that I'm sorry, Hugo, so terribly sorry . . .'

A heavy silence fell over the room, a pall weighted with regret, with mourning for hopes destroyed, for the waste of many precious hours.

The sound of a breath rasping from Hugo's throat startled her bent head erect so that she was gazing straight into dark, expressionless eyes when he confirmed the wrong she had committed.

'It is a woman's nature to employ regret as a penance, just as it is a man's to absolve himself from blame by pleading ignorance. In this instance, however, I must be honest and confess that I'm sorry too.'

CHAPTER TWELVE

'There is nothing love cannot face, there is no limit to its faith, its hope, its endurance!' The priest who had officiated at their marriage ceremony had been wrong, Tarini concluded, tightening her fists

around the handrail of the chairlift carrying her to the summit of the mountain. A shudder racked her cringing frame when the sun dipped behind cloud and a cold gust of wind caught her unawares. She no longer had faith; no hope for a marriage doomed to failure. The limit of her endurance had been reached the moment she had discovered herself incapable of facing the prospect of an evening in the company of an angry, disillusioned husband and the elegant Alpine beauty who, had she not been usurped, would have made a superbly sophisticated consort. So like a coward she had run from her responsibilities, had slipped out of the castle when Hugo's back was turned in an attempt to seek a solution to their dilemma among the peaceful mountains.

'*Guten abend*, Countess!' A voice she did not recognise, the grasp of an unfamiliar hand, jolted her back to earth when her chair reached the platform adjacent to a small café situated almost at the summit of the mountain.

'Good evening,' she responded with a blush, made aware for the very first time of being in the public eye, a personage who, to locals, had become instantly recognisable. 'Where is Hans?' she enquired of the young man whose blue eyes and blond hair fitted him into a category rarely seen in Alpine communities.

'He's not feeling well, so when customers began disappearing from the café—as they always do once the mountains begin frowning—I offered to take his place. I wanted to escort him to his home, but he refused my help and made off towards his chalet about an hour ago. Luckily, it is not far from here. In fact, if you step this way, Countess, you can see smoke curling from his chimney.'

Tarini hesitated. She had intended making her way to the valley of gentians, but Hans, her one close friend, could be in need of help.

'I don't like to think of him alone and probably in pain—do you think he would mind if I paid him a visit?'

'On the contrary, Countess, I'm sure he would be delighted,' the young man responded with the sort of gallantry she had become accustomed to receiving from every Liechtenstein male—except one!

'Over the years, Hans has become resigned to the fact that warmth, rest, and an occasional pain-killing tablet form the best remedy to combat the effects of rheumatism—an affliction imposed upon most veteran skiers—nevertheless, he still grumbles whenever the need to nurse painful joints cuts him off from society, therefore your company will be regarded as a welcome break from tedium. But you would be wise to make your visit a brief one,' he frowned upwards at puffball clouds drifting to form a pale grey necklace around the highest peak. 'The weather is threatening to change, and though it may blow over, the risk of being lost in a sudden fall of mist is too great to be ignored.'

But Tarini's eyes were fastened upon the curl of smoke rising from the chimney of a house looking, even at a distance, as typically Alpine as its owner—a structure consisting of horizontal tree trunks piled one on top of the other, its small windows flanked by bright green shutters, its stretch of balcony daubed with the fresh green foliage and bright red petals of flowering geraniums.

'I'll take care,' she absently acknowledged his warning, already treading the path leading up to the chalet tucked cosy as a nest upon a mountain ledge, 'please don't worry on my account—I've often wandered up here during early evening when there are still a few daylight hours to spare.'

Without the usual spring to her step, her usual wide-eyed air of interest, she plodded up the incline deep in thought, estimating that in less than an hour's time Hugo would saunter into her bedroom expecting to find a meekly submissive wife ready to be escorted to the hotel where they were both supposed to dine. She winced when imagination played a trick upon her senses, filling her ears with the thunder of slowly-rising wrath and closed her eyes to shut out the image of a profile etched stern as the face of the Eiger with jagged forks of lightning reflecting in the depths of ice-cold torrents.

Her footsteps quickened to scale the last stretch of incline as if some devil were yapping at her heels, then she stood for a moment to regain her composure before knocking on the herringbone-panelled door.

'Herein!'

Timidly she responded to the grunted command to enter by lifting the latch and stepping inside a spacious room obviously serving as a living-room, kitchen and bedroom combined, with walls of plain wood supporting a beamed, vaulted ceiling; cupboards, door surrounds and window frames made unique with skilful carving. A narrow, deep dresser stood against one wall and high-backed benches were ranged around the remaining three, with a small cabinet containing a handbasin fitted with pewter taps tucked into an alcove near the door. But the item that most caught her interest was a stone, barrel-shaped stove with smoke escaping through tiny elevated windows straight on to a smoke-blackened ceiling.

'Countess!' With an expression depicting surprised dismay, Hans struggled to rise out of his chair.

'Oh, please don't get up!' Tarini hurried across to him, alarmed by his gasp of pain when he attempted to exert pressure upon stiff, painful joints.

'Why are you walking alone in the mountains on a day such as this when all signs are pointing to unsettled weather?'

'Don't worry, Hans,' she attempted to soothe, 'the young man in charge of the chairlift has already warned me not to linger. I promised I'd stay just long enough to ensure that you have everything you need and to enquire about your health.'

'The young *dummkopf*!' Weakly, Hans slumped back into his chair. 'He ought to have known better than to even allow you to leave the chairlift, should have returned you to the lower reaches without delay. I had expected even a "newcomer" would have that much sense, otherwise I would not have allowed him to take over my duties!'

'The young man seemed very efficient,' her eyebrows elevated, 'in no way did he strike me as being a stranger to these parts.'

Hans grunted. 'He is one of a number of blue-eyed, fair-haired peasantry, wanderers from Switzerland, who settled in our area about six hundred years ago. According to legend, they had been driven from their homeland by famine. They acquired lonely farms and high, uncultivated lands similar to those they had left behind, and to this day they remain a race apart, speaking their own dialect, carrying out their own customs—such as refusing to sleep on mattresses, preferring instead to use beech leaves which they collect each autumn to use as bedding.'

'Six hundred years since they first settled here,' she gasped, 'and still you regard them as strangers!'

'They are not of our blood,' he shifted uncomfortably, then winced as if suffering a twinge of pain. 'Noble and common blood may be of the same colour, but there is a natural aristocracy among Liechtensteiners which discourages integration with foreigners—even though they be near neighbours—less our lineage should become weakened.'

'In that case,' she concluded bleakly, 'everyone must disapprove of their Count marrying an English girl?'

'*Nein, nein,*' Hans glared, outraged, 'all are agreed that Count Hugo has chosen well, that he has gained himself a wife who is natural, wholesome, contented and no doubt happiest in a house filled with children. It was with that thought in mind,' he confided slyly, 'that I began working on a belated wedding present.' Bending with difficulty over the side of his chair, he hauled on to his lap a wooden trough-shaped object which at first sight Tarini did not recognise. But when the heartshaped cut-outs, rockers delicately painted with fertility symbols, and a Crucifixion group carved into the canopy, finally registered a painful blush dispersed her expression of sweet solemnity. 'It is natural for a mother to wish to commend her new-born baby to the special protection of God,' Hans mused, his gnarled fingers tracing an inscription etched at the foot of the wooden cradle. *'May God Protect Thee,'* he translated. Then, obviously enjoying her confusion, he concluded with inoffensive earthiness, 'And pray that my stiff old fingers will recover their skill so that the cradle may be finished in time to welcome the arrival of the new heir of Triesen. But meanwhile, Countess,' he hastened to change the subject when, instead of the smile he had expected, her mouth betrayed an uncontrollable quiver, 'I have for you a "lovers'" case which you may find useful for storing small treasures.'

The little painted box with a hinged lid, padded and lined with deep green velvet, fitted comfortably into her palm.

'As the decorative work will reveal, Countess, it was made as a courtship present by a young man wanting his beloved to be reminded of him whenever she used it.'

Observing the faint clouding of his expression, the wistful look in old eyes reflecting the resurgence of half-forgotten memories, her grasp tightened around the gift she sensed was precious to him.

'You made this box, didn't you, Hans? For some girl you loved dearly . . .?'

'My late wife,' he admitted gruffly, 'the only girl I've ever known with eyes as blue as your own, Countess. All the large items you see in this room,' with a wave he indicated the bed, chest and wardrobe all carved and painted to a uniform design, 'were contributed by my bride as part of her dowry. But everything else I made with my own two hands, because my tongue tripped clumsily over words of endearment and I needed to find some other method of expressing my love. I've often wondered,' he sighed, then suddenly raised his head to question hopefully: 'Tell me, could any man, however mute and seemingly uncaring, keep his love secret from the woman to whom he is wed?'

Tarini's tear-blurred eyes roved over ladles and colanders with decorative handles; small containers for the daily requirements of salt and flour together with the spoons inside of them, made beautiful with chip carving; rosettes and flowers, animals and birds appliquéd with a loving hand to turn ordinary, everyday kitchen utensils into works of art so appealing no recipient bride would consider exchanging them for the splendid, impersonal treasures cramming the interior of Wolke Castle.

'It's the intention behind the gift, not its face value, that a woman considers most important, Hans.' She swallowed hard, the reminder of costly rings of a blood-red ruby pendant, jabbing sharp as a hook into her heart. 'I'm certain your wife must have felt greatly blessed, knowing every gift she received contained a little of yourself.'

A distant rumble of thunder disturbed their melancholy, a sound that brought the old man sharply back from the past into awareness of the present. 'Did you hear that?' He cocked his head to one side, tensely listening. 'Please, Countess, you must make off home immediately, if you delay a moment longer you will risk being soaked to the skin. Oh, if only I were able to escort you!' he exploded. 'Sometimes I go for weeks, months even, without suffering so much as a twinge, yet today of all days I am cursed with a crippling disability.'

'That's probably due to the fact that rheumy joints are very susceptible to changes in the weather,' she soothed, rising calmly to her feet. 'As you seem to find my presence disturbing, I'd better go. Don't try to get up,' she admonished sharply, 'and don't dare to struggle across to the window when I leave! Goodbye, dear Hans,' she stooped to kiss his weathered cheek, 'I'll call again as soon as I can—probably tomorrow.'

The sky had darkened, and as she began descending the narrow path the breeze, ever present at the summit, felt several degrees cooler. She shivered and buttoned up the fine white cardigan which had always provided sufficient warmth during her excursions, belatedly remembering Hugo's warning when he had condemned her predilection for solitary hikes.

'In no other region of the earth are creatures subjected to such severe selective conditions as in the high mountains. Only an expert, conditioned to the extraordinary changes that take place, hour by hour, day by day, season by season; to the climatic conditions; to the sudden change in temperature from hot to cold; to merciless storms; to difficult terrain in which there is perpetual danger from falling stones and avalanches, could hope to survive any prolonged exposure!'

But by the time she reached the platform where double lines of cable were clanking empty chairs down to the valley and back to the summit in perpetual motion, the sun was once again beaming, the threat of rain dispersing as quickly as clouds racing across clear blue sky towards the far horizon.

Indecisively, she lingered, eyeing the path leading up to the café where Hans' temporary assistant was no doubt busily engaged carrying out his normal duties.

'Liechtenstein males,' she murmured to herself, 'have a tendency to be over-protective towards those they still chivalrously term the weaker sex!' As she basked in sunshine, breathed in air so calm it was undisturbed by so much as a lazily-flapping wing, her certainty grew that the warnings she had received had been unnecessarily alarmist. Almost without volition, she sauntered towards the path leading to the valley of gentians, then quickened her steps, pretending not to have heard the shouted protest issuing from the direction of the café.

After five breathless minutes she slowed her pace, conscious of having been swallowed into a landscape mazed with twisting paths branching in various directions, outcrops of rock, almost vertical inclines, and shoulder-high thickets of dwarf pines.

She had been wandering for over an hour and was happily engaged searching through cushions of sedge plants for a glimpse of the starry white edelweiss that fought to preserve its existence by hiding away in spots inaccessible to the plucking fingers of thoughtless tourists, when a raindrop large as a coin splashed on to her forearm. Fearfully, she looked up and saw clouds marshalling fierce as troops around glowering peaks. Then as if at a click of a switch the sun disappeared and she was rooted to the spot by a terrifying clap of thunder. When lightning ripped the sky wide open she began running scared as a rabbit, first one way then the other without any definite motivation, her frightened eyes scouring the landscape for some niche that might offer protection from rain that began as a shower, then escalated within minutes to the volume of water spilling from an upturned bucket.

Her teeth were chattering, her clothes a sodden weight around her limbs, by the time she spied a rock overhanging a space just big enough to accommodate her shivering body. Thankfully she crawled inside, closing squeamish ears to a rustling that seemed fair indication that other small, panic-stricken creatures had taken refuge in the surrounding bushes.

But after an aeon of miserable discomfort, while rain hammered persistently upon the ground and a chill wind probed her hideout turning her hands and feet numb, her sodden clothes into a second ice-cold skin, she ceased caring about whether her four-footed companions were badger, marmot, or

Alpine hare, would have welcomed even closer proximity to any warm, furry body.

It would have been difficult to assess exactly when daylight faded, but in any case it did not matter, because by the time night had cast its shroud over storm-darkened mountains she had been overcome by a semi-conscious state of euphoria. A smile tugged at the corners of stiff lips tinged with blue when she imagined she could hear in the far distance the tinkling of a cowbell hung around the neck of a peacefully grazing animal.

Was the 'little weakling' wandering alone somewhere nearby? she wondered, experiencing a stealing sensation of warmth. And was she happy, as happy as she had felt herself the day she had walked at the head of a procession with a ruby-red accolade of triumph hung around her neck?

The cosy warmth of her body was making her feel drowsy, but she struggled against sleep, wanting to savour for a few more precious seconds the memory of a weakling bride dressed in wedding finery, parading up a long, long aisle. She had almost reached the altar when Hugo's face swam before her eyes, then was suddenly blanked from her vision.

'Hugo!' she moaned, then began struggling to free herself from unseen hands that were dragging her away from the spot where he had been standing. 'No, *no*,' she pleaded fretfully, 'leave me, please, I *want* to stay!'

Suddenly her feeble struggles ceased when through a void of darkness Hugo's voice penetrated, deep, weary, defeated as a man who had reached the end of his endurance.

'Wake up, Tarini! You are safe now, I promise you will never have cause to run away again!'

All she wanted was to be left to sleep, but some cruel devil kept jolting her awake, kept insisting that she should open her eyes and walk. When she was set forcibly upon her feet and supported within a tight circle of arms the agony of stiffness in her legs and feet was unbearable at first, then gradually it began to subside. Heat from a body holding her in such close proximity she felt pinned to a muscled chest emitting warmth and the dull, racing throb of a frantically beating drum had just begun penetrating her frozen skin when the blast of a whistle pierced her eardrums and a few seconds later three distant blasts signalled a reply.

Six blasts, a pause, then the three answering blasts continued until her ears were singing with the noise forming part of the torture inflicted by the tormentor who sadistically persisted in dragging her back and forth, who steeled her upright when her weak limbs threatened to fold, who kept up a continuous barrage of words that her mind was too befuddled to decipher, a ribbon of rhetoric that imposed a restrictive band around the curtain of sleep.

Weak tears of resentment were rolling down her cheeks by the time an army of loud-voiced men with dazzling torches and heavy, crunching boots invaded her dream.

'Fetch the stretcher!'

She heard the snap of a familiar voice before arms soared her body upward, then lowered it gently on to a sea of blissful oblivion.

After what seemed to have been a long, peaceful journey she surfaced to the feel of water lapping her chin and before opening her eyes she stretched luxuriously, enjoying the fanciful notion that her weary limbs were submerged in warm, creamy milk. Pleasurably contented, she struggled to lift weighted lids until they were far enough apart to allow a sideways peep through lashes smudged dark as bruises across wan cheeks.

'Your habit of stealing covert glances always makes me suspect you of having just done something terribly naughty, Tarini,' a steady, mild-mannered voice accused.

Lashes startled as sparrows' wings flew upwards so that wide, perplexed eyes could rove, first over Hugo, sitting mere inches away, his expression calm, his watchful eyes inscrutable, then around the room containing a barrel-shaped stove emitting waves of warmth; a decorative bed, wardrobe and chest of drawers; a smoke-blackened ceiling, in which she had made her farewells to Hans many hours ago. But the shock that jolted crimson flags of colour into her cheeks was the realisation that she was wallowing up to her chin in warm soapy water, being bathed like an infant in the huge, wooden half-cask, decorated around its entire circumference, that Hans had explained was a bride tub that formed a traditional part of every girl's wedding dowry.

'Do you mind?' Negligently—so negligently her vanity bridled—Hugo nodded towards the pile of sodden clothing lying discarded upon the floor.

'Someone had to do it, and as there was no woman available the task naturally fell to me. I did not think you would object,' he continued drily, steady eyes quizzing the accelerating spurt of colour turning her pale cheeks crimson. 'After all, we are far from being strangers to each other's naked bodies.' To her relief, he rose to his feet and reached for a huge white towel which he unfolded, then held like a cloak, inviting her to sidle into its folds. 'Outraged modesty seems to have had the desired effect—judging from your fiery cheeks, both temperature and circulation are now back to normal. Come,' impatiently he twitched the towel when she made no move to abandon the bride tub, 'you have been in there long enough, the water is bound to be cooling.'

He made no attempt to spare her embarrassment by looking away but kept his impersonal glance trained her way while, after struggling towards the conclusion that she had no other choice, she levered her slightly-rounded body out of the water and rushed to hide her confusion inside the towel's soft embrace. Immediately his arms closed around her she began trembling, but when he sat down, holding her swaddled like an infant in his lap, tiredness overwhelmed her and with a smothered yawn she leant her head, contented as a drowsy child, upon his chest.

'Why are you wearing an evening shirt under your sweater?' she murmured, lying completely relaxed, warm and dry within the circle of his arms.

'I did not have time to change.' For the very

first time his air of calm was betrayed by the tight snap to his voice when he continued: 'I had only just become aware of your absence from your room when I received a telephone call from the proprietor of the mountain café informing me that you had just been spotted making your way into the mountains, in spite of the fact that a storm was brewing.'

When he reached for a mug of warm milk Tarini was mildly surprised to see a tremor in fingers closing around the handle, causing the mug to jerk and splashing a few drops of milk on to the surface of the table.

'Here, drink this before you fall asleep.'

Trained to obedience since childhood, she dutifully drained the mug, then handed it back empty.

'Hold up your head a second.' With a corner of the towel he dabbed the milky residue from around her mouth, seeming more aggravated by the sight than by any he had encountered during his night of trauma. 'There are times, Tarini, when I'm undecided whether you should be kissed or spanked!'

His sigh held a note of resignation she found puzzling, but she dismissed it from her mind in her eagerness to learn of the events leading up to her rescue.

'Then what did you do?' she prompted, snuggling closer into a shoulder which, whether because of the soothing effects of the milk drink, or because of delayed reaction to her ordeal, had become suddenly representative of a haven.

'I raised the alarm to summon the help of the

mountain rescue team, then accompanied by most of the able-bodied males in the area—and one not so able who would listen to no arguments about the drawbacks imposed upon his agility by the crippling effects of rheumatism—we began scouring the mountainside for a slip of a girl who seems to have won the affections of the entire population of Liechtenstein.'

Casually, he dismissed the effort involved in an operation carried out in pitch darkness, the dangers that had faced men whose knowledge of the mountains had made them no less immune to the perils of slippery paths, falling rocks, and the certainty that one unwary step could send them toppling into a storm-blanketed crevasse. Yet out of the corner of one sleepy eye Tarini could see a jawline that looked carved from granite and one telltale pulse hammering at the edge of his chiselled mouth.

'Some instinct told me that you had made towards the valley of gentians,' he told her bleakly. 'I must have passed the spot where you were lying, because when I began retracing my steps my foot crushed some object I realised was not stone, so I shone my torch upon the ground to investigate and discovered the remains of a small painted box lined with velvet lying adjacent to what I had mistakenly assumed to be one of the few remaining patches of winter snow—but which actually turned out to be your white cardigan.'

He was holding her so close it was hard to decide whether the shudder that shook them both had originated in his body or her own.

'Where is Hans now?' she murmured, concerned about the old man deprived of his home comforts.

'As we dared not attempt transporting you down the mountain while the storm was still raging, he insisted upon letting us have the use of his chalet while he spends the rest of the night with friends.'

Easily, he rose to his feet and strode to deposit her, still cocooned within the towel, gently upon the bed. 'I think it is safe to allow you to close your eyes now, sleepyhead.' Flickering lamplight cast shadows over his devil-dark profile as he leant to study her sweetly-flushed face, yet he had never sounded less satanic when he continued huskily: 'Dream contented dreams, Tarini. Tomorrow you should be feeling well enough to return home, first to Wolke Castle, then to the only home where you are ever likely to find peace—in England.'

CHAPTER THIRTEEN

'I DON'T believe it!' The old Countess hissed, glaring as if holding Tarini solely responsible for the threatened smirch upon the Triesen family name. 'Hugo would never agree to such a course of action—he has often said that he regards divorce as an admission of failure, and my son has never failed in any of the ventures he has undertaken in the past!'

'But he was not wholly enthusiastic about marrying me in the first place,' Tarini reminded her gently. 'If you remember, Countess, our marriage was designed to supply you with companionship during your many bouts of illness. Unfortunately, neither Hugo nor I was blessed with sufficient foresight to even suspect the rapid improvement we have witnessed practically since the day of our wedding.'

Even the old lady who had been guilty of such lack of conscience in her determination to achieve her ends had the grace to blush. 'Perhaps I did dramatise my symptoms on occasions,' she had the effrontery to confess, 'but I am not ashamed of having resorted to underhand means in a bid to ensure my son's happiness. Yet having said that,' her shoulders lifted to adopt a bearing of great dignity, 'I would remind you that my health is not good and that shocks such as the one you have just administered are bound to react badly upon my suspect heart.'

The Countess had returned home just in time to join Tarini for lunch on the terrace. Hugo had left the castle earlier that morning—as he had done every day of the two weeks that had elapsed since he had dragged her half-frozen body from what might have become her mountain tomb—and he was not due to return until late evening. Even now, it was hard to believe that she had been offered what he had termed her 'release from an ill-fated coupling', and though she had winced at his choice of phrase, could she argue with the fact that marriage to a man in love with another woman had been doomed to failure from its outset? They had both suffered for their mistake, Hugo most of all—

especially yesterday, when he had called her into his study to tell her, tight-lipped, and obviously deeply conscious of offending against tradition: 'My solicitor has begun drawing up papers for our divorce. Although fully aware that it was undiplomatic, to say the least, for us to be seen to be still living together, I did not want you to leave until I felt certain that you had fully recovered from your ordeal. However, to repeat the legal phrase that was used, I have been told that we must cease "co-habiting". My solicitor has suggested that you should return to England as soon as possible—preferably tomorrow.'

Hiding a wince of pain, Tarini leant across the table to plead with heartbreak in her eyes. 'After I've gone, you won't try to make things more difficult for Hugo, will you, Countess? Please, if you feel any love at all for your son, show it by being supportive and understanding, by accepting the fact that his happiness depends upon Baroness Frick sharing his future.'

'Never!' The Countess almost swept a cup from the table in her agitation. 'You may have no objection to that woman stepping into your shoes, but I certainly have! I *know* you are in love with him, child,' suddenly her proud expression crumbled, baring the first crack Tarini had ever seen in her iron control. 'I simple cannot understand how you can be so spiritless,' she quavered, 'why you are allowing your husband to be stolen from you without putting up a fight!'

Tarini blinked, trying to erect a feeble dam against a rush of hot tears. 'It was you who christened me so aptly,' she choked. 'How can a weakling ever hope to outmatch the appeal of a true Alpine beauty?'

'She might, if she found courage enough to try,' the Countess pleaded, suddenly looking many years older than her age. 'Your looks have improved as greatly as your health since your arrival in Liechtenstein, your pretty face is rounded, your soft, gentle eyes would become truly irresistible if only they could find a sparkle, and there is a definite curvaceous attraction about your body. Undoubtedly, you will always appear fragile, but fragility appeals strongly to the protective instinct possessed by very masculine men—an urge to cosset and support which they are well aware would never be fully appreciated by any self-assured, sophisticated female. Be guided by one who speaks from experience, I beg of you, Tarini! Every man is to be had one way or another; don't be afraid to flirt with your husband, to practise all the tricks of coquetry. And most important of all to remember—fire won't flare without friction!'

Feeling too emotionally drained to reply, Tarini mumbled some excuse to the Countess and retreated from the terrace and the persistent arguments of the old lady who was too much a fighter ever to concede defeat. There was packing to be organised, the gathering up of treasured bits and pieces which, after her departure, would be all she had left to convince her that the happenings of the past few months had actually taken place and had not been merely a prolonged, wonderful daydream.

Yet she dallied at the far end of the terrace,

leaning her elbows upon a stone balustrade to gaze upward at the magnificent world of the Alps so that it could be firmly imprinted upon her memory. She had done so much, yet had left a great deal undone. An impulse to weep ached behind eyes that had no tears left to shed as she mourned being deprived for ever of the sight of Alpine roses gleaming in the setting sun; the sound of cowbells adding their benediction to Sunday Mass held in the open air, high in the mountains, so that the peasants who looked after the cattle were able to attend the service. Then, too, there was the poignant experience of listening to a yodelling voice ringing out over the valley at nightfall each evening, singing the ancient prayer of the cowherds. *'Oho, oho! Ave, ave, Maria . . . Be our protector from all beasts of prey! Lock the wolf's tooth, ban the bear's paw, Stop the roll of the stone, and the lynx's jaw, Bar the lion's path and the dragon's tail, Crush the raven's beak and the griffin's flail!'*

'You look pensive, Tarini, and a little sad. Is it because you are leaving Liechtenstein tomorrow without ever having found your valley of peace?'

She swung round, startled, her mind still dwelling upon beasts of prey, to face the man in whose veins ran the blood of romantic Celts, arrogant Romans and heathen Alemanics. She swallowed hard. 'I was regretting missing countless opportunities to buy a cuckoo clock and a miniature cowbell and alphorn.'

A scowl which recently had never seemed to be very far away darkened his features. 'You may choose from the contents of the castle anything which is likely to conjure happy memories of your stay here. The Countess von Triesen has no need to resort to buying trashy tourist souvenirs. Come,' his jaw clicked into arrogant rigidity as he stepped to one side, waiting for her to precede him, 'I'll help you to reach a decision. There are masterpieces by Rubens, Rembrandt, and Van Dyck that you might find appealing, plenty of tapestries and objets d'art, as well as a huge collection of family jewellery.'

'No, thank you, Hugo.' She hung her head. 'I shall have little use for any of the items you've just mentioned, nor any room to display them in the small flat I shall probably be sharing with my friend.'

'Don't be foolish!' Though she kept her eyes averted, his tone brought a forcible reminder of the lull she had mistaken for tranquillity just before the onset of the mountain storm. 'You must be aware that you will never again be in any danger of poverty, that you will receive an ample monthly allowance as well as——'

'No!' The cry sprang from her lips like a cry of pain, yet her wounded eyes cast a look of proud defiance. 'I refuse to accept any sort of payment for failure. The ... the happy memories,' she trembled, 'the many happy hours I've spent here are all the reward I need or deserve.'

'Together with the revenge gained from leaving behind a husband tortured by the knowledge that a previous Countess von Triesen may be starving in some attic? I think not, Tarini,' he emphasised with dangerous suavity. However, as it is unlikely that anything can be gained from further discussion we will leave all financial arrangements in the hands of our legal advisers. Now, as you no doubt wish to change,' he surprised her, sweeping a derogatory glance over her pink checked shirt and faded denims, 'I will wait for you by the car. I have a small business matter to attend to, and as you seem anxious to purchase toys you may accompany me to Vaduz.'

An atmosphere of unspoilt friendliness and courtesy prevailed throughout the capital of the tiny principality.

'Twenty policemen keep law and order throughout the land.' Hugo's aloofness relaxed into humour as he drove between narrow, immaculately-swept pavements thronged with local shoppers and groups of tourists gaping into shop windows displaying an assortment of goods guaranteed to excite the interest of anyone seeking something 'different'. 'Owing to the increasing weight of traffic, it has recently been suggested that the number should be raised to thirty. We can also boast one small jail, which luckily is nearly always empty.'

'Everyone looks so carefree and gay,' Tarini smiled, her spirits lifted by the sight of so many happy faces.

'We Liechtensteiners are normally possessed of a happy disposition,' he defended drily. 'Even the "Unterlanders" who have a reputation of being more careful with their francs than the "Oberlanders" who are particularly lighthearted—probably because they are to be located among the vineyards where much wine is known to flow. Nevertheless, cautious mothers often warn their daughters never to fall in love with a "frivolous Oberlander". In country districts young people look forward to autumn when the harvest is over. Then, men and girls meet each evening in various farmhouses to help strip off the leaves of the maize cobs. While working they sing and play games, but as soon as the work is finished a great feast begins, wine is drunk, and dancing continues until the early hours of the morning. These parties have been known to last a fortnight, by which time even the youngest and fittest are ready for a good night's sleep. You must taste the stew made of pork and beans——' He broke off, his lips tightening with annoyance at this slip of the tongue, but luckily his attention was diverted by their arrival at a car park so congested he had to negotiate carefully into one of the few remaining spaces left vacant.

'If you have no objection, I'll leave you to browse around the shops alone until I've concluded my business.'

Relief washed over Tarini as, guided by his hand cupping her elbow, she and Hugo began walking the few yards dividing the car park from the shopping centre.

'That will suit me fine,' she responded quickly, then blushed when his sharp glance indicated disapproval of what must have appeared to be an ill-mannered display of eagerness to be rid of him.

His tone held a hint of lingering displeasure when he left her outside a department store thronged with tourists. 'In here you will find everything, from cameras to postcards, diamond watches to cuckoo clocks. There is a café next door with tables set out on the pavement—if you have finished your shopping before I return go there and wait for me.'

When he strode off every female head in the vicinity turned to follow the progress of the man whose limbs—used to the rigours of athletic training—moved fluid as a mountain stag beneath a conventional, perfectly-tailored suit. A sense of loss descended upon Tarini, a weight so oppressive she could not concentrate upon the conglomeration of goods crammed upon counters, stacked upon shelves lining the tourist shop from floor to ceiling, so five minutes later she left the shop without having made a single purchase.

Disconsolately, lacking any sense of purpose, she wandered down streets and narrow lanes fronted with shops displaying local handicrafts and exotic, exciting wares from many different countries. The nightdress, when she saw it, stopped her in her tracks and drew her wide-eyed with wonder to peer closer into the window of a boutique flaunting the wicked creation in chiffon and lace, black as sin, with a neckline plunging low as a navel and lace-trimmed side slits reaching almost waist-high, a confection so diaphanous it lay draped, with room to spare, between the outstretched, silver-painted fingers of a dummy hand. Driven by some impulse she dared not wait to examine, she stepped towards the entrance, hesitated a second, then pushed open the door and stepped inside . . .

Hugo was already seated at a table when, flushed

and breathless, she arrived at the café where they had arranged to meet.

'I hope I haven't kept you waiting long?'

'You haven't,' he assured her, rising politely to his feet. 'I arrived only a few minutes ago. I have already ordered coffee—what would you like to go with it, an ice cream, or perhaps you would prefer a large slice of creamy gâteau?'

His avuncular tone set her teeth on edge, and somehow managed to make even greater nonsense of the hasty purchase that had been slid, soft as a sigh, into the parchment-thick, gaily scrolled bag, no larger than an envelope, that she was grasping in one tight fist.

'Why do you always treat me like a child, Hugo?' she burst impulsively.

'I don't—I haven't *always*,' he qualified meaningfully. Then as if regretting the intrusion of intimacy, he steered the conversation into less dangerous channels. 'What have you been buying?' His nod indicated the bag resting on her lap.

'A nightdress.'

Eagle-dark eyebrows winged skyward. 'Oh, of course,' he drawled, pretending sudden enlightenment, 'you will no doubt find more use for prim-collared, ankle-length sleeping shrouds now that you are reverting to modest spinsterhood.'

'It bears no resemblance to a shroud and it's far from prim!' Suddenly, the rankling deprivation of having been left to sleep alone ever since the night they had shared Hans' chalet, a night when more than any time before or since, she had needed the comfort of his strong arms around her, rioted out of control. Though kicking nerves had begun a dull, heavy pounding in her ears, though her stomach was churning and every modest instinct had shrivelled into a tight, protesting lump that had lodged in her throat, her brazen tongue seemed determined to startle Hugo into discarding the bland, spiceless diet of words he had doled in her direction until she felt choked.

'As you seem so interested in my purchase, why don't you satisfy your curiosity by coming to my room tonight when I shall be wearing it?'

Never had she expected to see the worldly, imperturbable Count look so shaken. After one bold glance lasting no longer than a second, she lowered her lashes, flinching from an ice-green stare that made her feel like a Jezebel.

His voice sounded strangled, every word laboured, when he censured: 'Circumstances being what they are, what you have just suggested is immoral, Tarini, and considering the advanced stage of our divorce proceedings, might even be illegal!' Her abasement hit rock bottom when he rose to his feet and clipped: 'I think we had better go, before any further amateurish attempt at verbal seduction manages to persuade me that anyone reckless enough to set doors wide open to a thief deserves to be robbed!'

He drove home in tight-lipped silence, with Tarini, her stomach knotted into a ball of shamed embarrassment, feeling too demoralised to even attempt conversation. As soon as they arrived at the castle she fled from his disapproval to seek sanctuary in her bedroom where, with her weak limbs stretched flat upon the bed, she lay shaking, trying to come to terms with the finality of his contemptuous rejection.

Many hours later she was aroused from her misery by a tap upon the door and a servant's voice informing her that dinner was ready to be served.

'Please convey my apologies to the Count and Countess,' she managed to husk loud enough for the servant to hear, 'and tell them not to wait as I shan't be joining them for dinner this evening.'

Mercifully, no one appeared to question her absence, probably, she brooded despondently, forcing herself to finish her packing, because already she had been condemned to the mists of obscurity. In less than a week she would have been forgotten, a timid English sparrow whose personality had left as little impression upon the arrogant Triesens as the cloud swirling, lingering, then drifting slowly past the turrets of Cloud Castle.

In a chair pulled close to an open window she watched the setting sun turn the blue sky orange, then pale pink shot with pearl, before night stole stealthily from the east to draw a mantle of black velvet spangled with stars. It seemed pointless undressing for bed, when she knew she would be unable to sleep. But because a dawn departure for Zürich airport made some kind of rest imperative, she reluctantly abandoned her chair and began forcing stiff fingers to struggle with buttons which suddenly seemed to have enlarged to twice the size of their buttonholes.

She had succeeded in slipping out of her clothes and was reaching for one of the modest nightdresses Hugo had so scathingly maligned when her glance fell upon the colourfully inscribed paper bag that she had dropped in passing upon her dressing table.

'Why not?' she murmured softly under her breath, sliding the nightdress, black as night shadows, through her outstretched fingers. 'This is one dream, at least, that can be turned into reality—albeit without an audience!'

A wicked thrill, shocking in its sensuality, followed the trail of black chiffon across her creamy skin. She glanced into a mirror, then gasped, averting her eyes as if ashamed of intruding into the privacy of a stranger whose naked body gleamed pale and rounded as the alabaster statue poised on a plinth in the night-shrouded garden. She was about to shrug it off, feeling the cling of black chiffon as unsuitable as an ill-fitting glove, when she faltered, then was drawn towards the aroma of tobacco smoke drifting past her open window. Just a few feet away, behind a door opening out on to a shared balcony, Hugo was obviously enjoying a last cheroot before retiring to bed unusually early.

Leaning heavily upon curtains clutched in a tight fist, she strained her ears for sounds of movement and heard only the pounding of her own heartbeats, felt the ache of a body that had dissolved entirely into one heavily throbbing pulse. 'Hugo, my darling,' she whispered into the still night air, 'I love you so much, how can I hope to survive the heartbreak of leaving you!'

With tear-filled eyes she stumbled outside on to

the balcony, and immediately became aware of a strong breeze whipping the branches of surrounding trees. Weakly, she tried to resist its pressure by leaning slightly backwards, then felt a gust contacting sharp as a blow behind her knees that knocked her off balance so that she staggered forward, straight into the arms of her surprised husband.

'Tarini! What the devil . . .!' Roughly he pulled her inside his room and closed double glass doors behind him. 'Are you anxious to court a chill?' he glowered, thrusting clenched fists deep into the pockets of a dark silk dressing-gown. 'Haven't you suffered enough from exposure without lingering on a chilly balcony dressed in nothing more substantial than . . . that——'

He broke off, obviously stunned by his first clear view of her appearance.

'Holy Saints,' he muttered hoarsely, 'whatever possessed you to mar your innocence with such a shocking garment?'

For some unknown reason, his savage dislike of the only sophisticated article of apparel she had ever owned struck at the heart of her pride, forcing an uncharacteristic spark of indignation.

'You wouldn't have said that if Baroness Frick had been wearing it!'

Visibly aggravated by the comparison, he pounced, his grip searing a brand of anger upon the soft, tender curve of each shoulder.

'You are not Baroness Frick—indeed you are her complete antithesis!'

'Gauche, plain and simple, I suppose you mean?'

Tarini gulped, betraying the first glint of tears he had ever seen her shed.

'No, Tarini,' he groaned, devouring her face with a look turned suddenly, unbelievably tortured, 'sweet, gentle, innocent—too sincere to be able to hide the revulsion you felt for a husband who forced you to risk your life in the mountains rather than suffer another night of his unwanted love-making. I would have wanted to die myself if anything had happened to you that night,' he confessed in a low, hoarse whisper that reacted upon her senses like a hymn of hope. 'As it was, I made a pledge to all the saints that if my prayers were answered I would release my captive sparrow and allow her to fly home.' Suddenly, he flung away from her and strode across to the window, leaving her staring mutely at the ripple of muscles knotting beneath silk stretching tightly across his shoulders. 'But you're making it very hard for me, Tarini,' he clenched, 'first with your very surprising invitation this afternoon and now this!'

'You want *me*?' Tarini pleaded, wondering if her mind had fallen victim to some blissful derangement. 'But . . . but how can you, when all I've ever managed to do is make you angry, angry enough to accuse me of interfering between yourself and Baroness Frick, of deliberately tricking you into marriage?'

'Yes, you have often made me angry,' he agreed without turning his head, 'an anger born of frustration because from the moment you erupted into my well-planned, free-and-easy existence the image of a pitiful waif with soulful blue eyes has dominated my thoughts to the exclusion of everyone else. A suspicion that you were destined to play a major role in my life became concrete the day I realised that I did not care—in fact, was enormously relieved—when Maria broke off our engagement. Yet I was unwilling to admit even to myself that I had become enslaved by a little weakling, right up until our wedding day.'

Slowly he turned to face the girl whose pale, slender body looked sculpted from marble to confess gravely.

'I can't tell you how much I regretted Maria's interference on our wedding day—the day I became resigned for the first time in my life to a depth of commitment to one woman that previously I had always carefully avoided. Many times, I've wondered how our relationship might have developed had Maria's possessive attitude not caused you to retreat into your shell, so that I was driven through fear of losing you, into trying to stamp my brand of ownership upon a dreamer who refused to be fully aroused, upon a bride whose dutiful, calm tolerance of brutal mastery almost drove me mad. It's been hell!' he exploded, looking ready to bundle her out of his sight, 'hammering on the door of love you've kept firmly shut!'

Relieved of the weight of a thousand pains, Tarini stared at the tyrant who had suddenly exposed his chains, the slavish chains of love that should have held them together but which instead had pulled them apart.

'*Hugo darling*,' she almost sobbed, 'if it's true that there can be no peace of mind in love, we must be destined to share a very turbulent life-time!'

She flew into arms that opened tentatively to receive her, offered her lips to be kissed to a man who held back because he had suffered too much to risk a further rebuff.

'*I love you*, my darling,' she whispered, enticing his trust with a look that reflected everything he had taught her about the art of seduction, then gloried in the crush of arms that snatched her tightly as the fragile, indestructible edelweiss clings to its native rock.

'I can't promise you contentment, *liebchen*,' he warned hoarsely, 'nor a placid existence. All I can offer is the heartbreak of being jealously guarded, closely cosseted, and loved to distraction!'

Eyes blue as wild gentians adored the mountain Adonis who, when racing on skis down snow-covered slopes, would look like an eagle soaring.

'One miracle is sufficient in anyone's lifetime, my darling,' she sighed. Then enchanting him with the sight of an errant dimple, she teased softly: 'After all, a surfeit of happiness can be fatal, as was proved by one other, far less fortunate "little weakling"!'

Harlequin® Plus

A WORD ABOUT THE AUTHOR

Margaret Rome's first Harlequin was published in 1969. Appropriately, it was entitled *A Chance to Win* (Harlequin Romance #1307).

But her chance was a while in coming. In her teens Margaret dealt with a long-term bout of rheumatic fever; then followed a series of manual jobs that "just could not satisfy my active mind," and finally marriage and the birth of a son. But at last, when Margaret did get down to the business of writing—beginning by doodling with pen and paper—she discovered that a sentence formed, a second one followed, and before long, paragraphs had developed into a chapter. "I had begun the first of many journeys," she says.

Today Margaret and her husband make their home in Northern England. For recreation they enjoy an occasional night out dancing, and on weekends they drive into the beautiful Lake District and embark on long, invigorating walks.

Harlequin
Romances

A Bowl
of Stars
A Parade
f Peacocks
On a
May Morning

Choose from this list of Harlequin Romance editions.*

975 **Sister of the Housemaster**
Eleanor Farnes
978 **Kind and Gentle Is She**
Margaret Malcolm
991 **Charity Child**
Sara Seale
1150 **The Bride of Mingalay**
Jean S. MacLeod
1152 **A Garland of Marigolds**
Isobel Chace
1154 **You Can't Stay Here**
Barbara Gilmour
1157 **Yesterday's Magic**
Jane Arbor
1158 **The Valley of Aloes**
Wynne May
1159 **The Gay Gordons**
Barbara Allen
1164 **Meadowsweet**
Margaret Malcolm
1165 **Ward of Lucifer**
Mary Burchell
1166 **Dolan of Sugar Hills**
Kate Starr
1171 **The Wings of Memory**
Eleanor Farnes
1174 **The English Tutor**
Sara Seale
1176 **Winds of Enchantment**
Rosalind Brett
1178 **Rendezvous in Lisbon**
Iris Danbury
1182 **Golden Apple Island**
Jane Arbor
1189 **Accidental Bride**
Susan Barrie
1190 **The Shadow and the Sun**
Amanda Doyle
1193 **The Heights of Love**
Belinda Dell
1197 **Penny Plain**
Sara Seale
1199 **Johnny Next Door**
Margaret Malcolm
1211 **Bride of Kylsaig**
Iris Danbury
1212 **Hideway Heart**
Roumelia Lane
1226 **Honeymoon Holiday**
Elizabeth Hoy
1228 **The Young Nightingales**
Mary Whistler
1233 **A Love of Her Own**
Hilda Pressley
1246 **The Constant Heart**
Eleanor Farnes
1494 **The Valley of Illusion**
Ivy Ferrari
1605 **Immortal Flower**
Elizabeth Hoy

*Some of these book were originally published under different titles.